PRAISE FOR KATE AXELROD

"Axelrod's prose is careful, intelligent, and contemplative…"

—PUBLISHERS WEEKLY

"The perfect stories for reanimating your soul when you've gone numb online but still yearn to engage with the human condition."

—ELISA ALBERT, AUTHOR OF *HUMAN BLUES*

"The stories in *How to Get Along Without Me* are wary and beautiful, savage and true. Kate Axelrod has given us a book that is both modern and timeless."

—LINDSAY HUNTER, AUTHOR OF
HOT SPRINGS DRIVE

"Viciously funny and unashamedly sexy stories that plumb the loneliness of desire from first swipe to coupledom."

—DANIELLE LAZARIN, AUTHOR OF *BACK TALK*

"Surprising, funny, and painfully true. *How to Get Along Without Me* is an anthropological account of dating, a catalogue of shitheads, a love letter to grandparents, and a reminder that those years of flailing in love and failing to launch are 'taut with possibility.'"

—CHRISTINE SMALLWOOD, AUTHOR OF *THE LIFE OF THE MIND*

"Kate Axelrod's brilliant stories of love and lust in the big city made me both nostalgic for and grateful to be long past my own reckless New York youth. Sharp, poignant, and full of perfect details, this is a debut to remember."

—ANDREW MARTIN, AUTHOR OF *EARLY WORK*

"I love interconnected short stories and I loved the stories in Kate Axelrod's collection *How to Get Along Without Me*. Axelrod has the gift of creating characters who seem so very much like either people I know or who I once was back when I was a person who went on dates."

—MARCY DERMANSKY, AUTHOR OF *HURRICANE GIRL*

HOW TO GET ALONG
WITHOUT ME

KATE AXELROD

HOW TO GET ALONG
WITHOUT ME

For Andrew, Amaia and Julian

And in loving memory of Bill Block

"The past, like a sudden tide, had swept back over him, not as it had been but as he could not help remembering it."

—JAMES SALTER, "BANGKOK"

CONTENTS

THEIR EXES' EXES

Josh

Ashley's birthday was on April 20th, the same day as Hitler's and Columbine and obviously four-twenty, which you observed like a national holiday. Her mother's name was Marilyn and her family lived on Marilyn Place. Ashley was a really beautiful poet, you said. She loved Dar Williams and sometimes you'd see her in the hallways and she'd be writing song lyrics on the white rubber of her Converse. You were crazy about her. You took Valium together and passed out on the blacktop of your driveway. Her dad had died the year before and the world was fuzzy through her grief. She pawed at you messily. *I'm right here,* you wanted to tell her.

Jack

You and Maggie shared a room in your college co-op where there were communal meals and a hammock strung up inside the common room, and someone was always baking loaves of bread in the middle of the night.

You thought you spent all your time together but somehow it wasn't enough. One Saturday night, Maggie wanted to stay in and watch *Breathless*. You texted her in the afternoon, told her your friends had spiked your lunch with shrooms. You said you were pissed but decided to roll with it. The next day she confronted your friends and they laughed, told her the entire thing was your idea. Sometimes she reminded you of that Dylan line, I gave her my heart but she wanted my soul.

Charlie

On your seventeenth birthday, Haley gave you a blowjob in the stairwell of her parents' building on 97th and Amsterdam. You met in AP History and she had the biggest tits you'd ever seen. You joked that you wanted to tattoo each of her breasts; one would say *Charlie's* and the other would say *Property*. You both applied early to Brown and she got in, and you ended up at Oberlin. During Thanksgiving break, you told her you applied to transfer and she said, *I'm sorry but please, please, please don't.*

Jamie

Amy's favorite candies were Reese's Pieces and on Valentine's Day you bought a bunch of king-sized bags and emptied them all out into her single, extra-long dorm bed. It was supposed to be romantic and playful but she was annoyed for weeks, finding pieces of crushed candy stuck to her sheets.

Dean

Lizzie's dad was a real piece of shit. He left when she was four and popped up periodically, sending change of address cards when he moved from New Jersey to Florida to Colorado. Once, when he visited New York, you all went out for dinner at a Chinese restaurant in Midtown. Each time Lizzie started to serve herself some lo mein or chicken and cashews, he'd swing the Lazy Susan back around his way.

Gabe

Mona was your rock. She was in graduate school for global public health and once, when she went to Turkey for a few weeks, you got drunk and fucked a coworker in the bathroom at a bar in South Williamsburg. You were depressed, you said. You didn't even come, could barely stay hard, and you weren't planning to tell her but when you picked her up at the airport it just spilled out. *Wow,* she said, *I didn't think you were the kind of guy who couldn't handle being with a smart, ambitious woman.* That one really stuck with you.

Peter

You met Leila during your freshman year of college and she propelled you out of your upper middle-class suburban existence, took you to your first Jews for Palestine meeting at the student center. At Thanksgiving, you watched in awe as she went toe to toe with your Uncle Jerry, contesting stats about the occupation. You married on a frigid day in February at City Hall. She wore a blue dress and winter boots. Three years later she left you; said she grew out of the relationship, and maybe she didn't even believe in the institution of marriage at all. You tell me she's still one of your closest friends. We go to a bar in Park Slope with gleaming wooden floors and shuffleboard in the back. We drink Old Fashioneds and you tell me you'd like to make our relationship work, you just need to take things slowly. The next morning, we lie in bed watching a video of a deer in Montana eating a cupcake. A text arrives on your screen. It's from *Susan cell* and says, "thank you, love!!! Sixty-five is feeling great so far." Then comes a picture of Susan, who is smiling and holding two tiny Maltese up to the camera. You say Susan is your mother-in-law. *Former,* I whisper. *Right,* you say, swiping the picture up and away.

BOTH JOSHES

For a while when I was twenty-four, I was sleeping with two guys named Josh. They were both allergic to cats, but otherwise they were nothing alike. Josh L was earnest and always wanted to "talk things out" or "process," and Josh K was sort of emotionally limited. He had difficulty exchanging affection.

My therapist, Sharon, had a field day with the fact that they were both allergic to cats, because I had grown up with cats and currently had one named Sally, who was a longhaired Persian with bright blue eyes and tan fur who shed constantly. My furniture and clothing were covered in a sheath of pale fur, so much so that I had given up wearing dark colors. Sometimes Josh L would sleep over even though Sally's fur was everywhere, all over the bed, and I'd hear him wheezing in the middle of the night. Meanwhile, Josh K would fuck me and before he even pulled out, would start coughing and say he was starting to feel allergic. Sometimes I'd ask if he wanted to take anything—I kept a carton of CVS brand antihistamines in my medicine cabinet—and he'd just say, "Nah, thanks though."

Sharon once asked me what it meant that I'd chosen to date two people who were "quite literally" allergic to my home. She probably wanted me to say that I was actively choosing men who couldn't be with me and creating scenarios where there was no hope of the relationship working out, as a way of protecting myself against rejection. But what the two Joshes meant to me was that way too many people were allergic to cats and maybe there should be a little more research about finding a cure.

Maia and I were twenty-four and living in LA, in an apartment south of Sunset in an L-shaped complex, with grey wall-to-wall carpeting and a terrace overlooking a small track. The complex was far from the beach and close to a lot of intersecting freeways and the set of a movie Maia was working on. We both wanted to work in "the biz." I wanted to act but really would've settled for anything acting adjacent. For three months I'd been standing on street corners in Brentwood with a clipboard and a blue ballpoint pen, asking people if they had a moment to support the DNC. Obama was running for his second term, but nobody I knew seemed concerned about his chances. (Later I'd feel nostalgic for that particular election, which didn't feel especially freighted with existential despair.) Most people walked right past us, some pretended to look for something in their bags, others stared intently at their phones. Once, outside a shopping center on San Vicente, Meg Ryan handed me a crisp ten-dollar bill.

In the afternoons, I'd go to Coffee Bean and Tea Leaf and drink Vanilla Iced Blendeds and look for jobs on Craigslist. I kept copying and pasting a generic cover letter, about my major in cinema studies and *my passion for the arts.*

I kept both Joshes in my phone under their last names because I didn't want to confuse the two in texting. Or actually, I came to suspect, because I didn't want to see the name JOSH on my phone and feel a flutter of excitement, before I registered which one it was.

I resented feeling like a cliché for wanting the unavailable guy, but the fact was, I really did truly like Josh K a lot. Any time I asked him a question about his day or tried to have a conversation with him about feelings, he would respond in all capital letters saying THE STRUGGLE IS REAL. But he'd made more than one reference to his parents' ugly divorce, and I had this sense that he was just protective because of the drama he must've witnessed as a kid. Maia always rolled her eyes when I said this. She named all the other people we'd known whose parents had split up but were able to commit and be regular, reasonable partners. Josh K was just more complicated than that, I supposed. He worked at a startup in Venice. I didn't know what exactly he did but it had something to do with solar panels, though he told me he was applying to law school and was hoping to end up "back east" before too long.

I'd met Josh L on OkCupid. He worked in film like everybody else and had two pictures on his profile: one was him in a darkened bar with floral wallpaper and a candle illuminating his face and the other was of him and a very little kid, sitting on a bench at the Santa Monica Pier. The kid was probably two, and Josh L was holding an ice cream cone up above her head as she reached for it adoringly. She had a pink scaly ring around her mouth and snot crusted below her nostrils.

The caption said, "love this girl. but not mine, niece!!" I swiped right because I thought it'd be good for me to like someone who was into kids.

It had recently been Yom Kippur and, with my family back on the East Coast, I'd decided to go to synagogue with one of my DNC coworkers. From across the country, my parents continued to parent in their distinct ways. My mother sent care packages with all natural sunscreens and dried fruit or chocolate covered nuts. My father called with reminders to get my oil changed or to make sure I filed my taxes on time. Sometimes he'd text me and ask that I please call my mother, because she had a doctor's appointment or a meeting at school that she was worried about.

At an airy reform synagogue on Beverly Glen, I tried to make a list of things I wanted to do better in the next year. One was, talk less shit about my mom. The other was, date guys who were into me.

When Josh L messaged me on OkCupid, I had already been seeing Josh K for about six weeks. Josh K and I had met at a bar in Culver City where Maia was going for a coworker's birthday. They were all dancing in the back and Josh K and I were lingering by this old school jukebox filled with pages and pages of CDs. I made a comment about how I hated dancing and was so relieved there was something else to do.

"Same," Josh K said. "I want to be the kind of person who dances and yet…"

We went back to my house and he went down on me for like twenty minutes and it felt really good in moments but also really boring. My mind kept drifting to things I needed to do, like pay my loans for the month or buy that new lavender scented litter I kept seeing at the supermarket.

I tried to guide his head away from my crotch. At one point I even said, "I want to fuck you right now," but he didn't seem to care. It was almost like he had made a bet and was determined to make me come so he wouldn't lose fifty bucks. Eventually, so that it would end, I started moaning and clenching the muscles around my thighs.

I was slightly in awe of myself whenever I faked orgasms. I knew some people thought it was just another tool of the patriarchy, giving men the satisfaction of thinking that they had gotten you off, but to me it was the opposite: I felt powerful and secretive, guarding a tiny part of myself, like a sparkling jewel at the end of a video game that's nearly impossible to capture.

Josh K looked at me triumphantly and then we slapped five. Afterward, we lay in bed and talked about how sad it was that there were no seasons in Los Angeles. Josh K was from New Jersey.

"It's so annoying that you're supposed to be happy all the time just because it's always nice out," I said.

"I know," Josh K said. "Like, those days back home where it's cold and grey outside and the perfect excuse to 'curl up with a good book on the couch.' You cannot do that shit here."

I felt something unfurling inside my chest—but then Josh K started sneezing and pretty quickly put on his jeans and his plaid shirt and ordered himself a taxi.

After that first time Josh K never reached out once. Whenever I texted to see if he wanted to hang out he always wrote back right away and said "ya" or gave the thumbs up emoji. If I just gave him a concrete, specific plan, he'd meet up with me wherever. But then every date was like the first date again. It was like going to the gynecologist at student health; it felt so intimate but then when I went back a couple months later, the doctor stared at me blankly, with no indication at all that she remembered my last appointment.

One Tuesday night in October I had a date with Josh L. We were watching *Homeland*. A couple weeks earlier he'd asked if I'd wanted to start it with him. The intimacy of committing to a TV show with him seemed totally premature, requiring a level of trust and sacrifice that I was not ready for. But I was also compelled by Claire Danes' frenetic energy and the soft paternal presence of Mandy Patinkin. He reminded me of my father, both of them had a quality that was simultaneously gruff and warm. I got hooked quickly. We had a pretty nice night together, but after we had sex I felt an inexplicable need for him to leave. I went to the bathroom and then tried to gently nudge Sally into my room so that maybe he would get wheezy and decide to leave. But he just leaned over, took a packet of Claritin from his backpack and placed it on the night table. "Just in case," he said, and kissed the side of my face.

That I was expected to like him just because he was a nice guy who took his niece to get ice cream and used *her pleasure* condoms when we fucked, filled me with a peculiar kind of rage. I pretended to fall asleep and then got up to smoke a joint out the living room window. Maia was passed out on the couch. *Friends* was playing on Netflix and Joey was dressed up in all of Chandler's clothes. I laughed and coughed at the same time, smoke spilled out of my mouth. Maia squirmed and when I kissed the top of her head, her eyelids fluttered open. Then Sally walked in circles between my legs, her tail brushing against my thighs. I put the joint out and picked her up. "Do you know how much I love you?" I asked her. She blinked at me several times.

The next day, Wednesday, I got a response from Billy —a "writer/producer" looking for an assistant. He said he was in the early stages of a production that was half *Fear and Loathing in Las Vegas* and half *Look Who's Talking*. I drove to his place the next morning. He lived on the edge of Koreatown in a peach-colored apartment complex. The intercom was a tangle of wires spilling out from the wall. I stood, trying to figure out what to do, but then he threw a single sock out the window. "The key's inside," he said.

When I got up the stairs, the door was ajar and Billy was reclining on a corduroy armchair. He had shoulder-length silver hair and was wearing cargo shorts and a Hawaiian t-shirt. He opened his mouth and placed a green Listerine sheet on the surface of his tongue.

"Casey," he said. "Have a seat."

I was wearing a two-toned dress from Nordstrom Rack that looked like it was a skirt and a shirt. I had my resume printed out in my lap, but it didn't say much. I'd done an acting/directing summer program in high school at a local community college, where I smoked cigarettes for the first time and watched a lot of Godard films. I had vague dreams of becoming an actress, but I wasn't ambitious or pretty enough to make myself stand out among all the beautiful women in LA who committed themselves to daily open casting calls or raw food diets.

Billy said my name very slowly, with a vague smile across his face. Maybe he was high or maybe this was just what people sounded like on the West Coast. "I just finished this great script and I'm looking for someone to help me with pitching. I need help calling agents and backers and stuff like that. We're pretty much looking for everyone: the actors, producers, PAs, everything."

"That's really exciting," I said. I told him how my experiences working for the DNC and my job in college making phone calls for the alumni office made me an excellent candidate. I was good at pitching, I felt comfortable asking people for money.

Then Billy led me down a short, carpeted hallway and into his office which was actually his bedroom. There was a chrome desk against the far wall, and several topless photos of Drew Barrymore—neatly hung and autographed—above it. Billy sat on a frameless king-sized bed, draped in paisley sheets. He gently patted the blanket beside him and asked me to have a seat. I declined, so he brought out a plastic fold out chair and positioned it beside the mattress.

"So, look," he said, "why don't we roleplay you pitching my screenplay to an agent. Here's a summary of the plot, you can look at it briefly and then try it on your own."

I took the summary from Billy but when I tried to read it the text was blurred together. I was shaking a little and my mouth was suddenly extremely dry, like I had just smoked an enormous joint.

"Are you okay?" he asked. "You seem pretty nervous. Do you need anything? I can heat you up a frozen dinner if you'd like."

It was 10:15 in the morning. I felt a swell of nausea. I figured that if I read the pitch for even a second, Billy would remove a flaccid penis from his cargo shorts, and begin to touch himself. I tried to focus on Drew Barrymore's lovely smile and buoyant tits, but I kept seeing Billy's pubic hair in my head, wiry and gray. I imagined his hand as he worked furiously toward an erection that would probably never materialize.

"You know what? I totally spaced and I realized I forgot to put money in the meter downstairs."

Billy sighed.

"I'll be back in two minutes," I said, reaching for my car keys. I held them up to him. A handful of keys was attached to a miniature yellow Converse high-top. I got in the car. It was an old Volvo that smelled like rotten licorice. I drove two blocks, made a right on Western and pulled over onto a small side street. It was sunny and I lowered the windows with the old-school manual crank. I let the heat pour in and the light sting my face. My heart was still hammering inside my chest, but I felt incredibly relaxed, almost gleeful. I pumped the lever beside my seat so that I was lying all the way back, basically horizontal.

I called Maia. She didn't pick up and then texted a minute later and said, "Who died or got engaged? Why are you calling? Text me like a regular person pls. Love you."

Then I called my mom, who was always delighted to hear from me. "Sweetie?" she said. "Casey?" I hung up immediately and then I texted her, "sorry, think i butt dialed you!!"

I would be two hours late for my DNC job, but it didn't matter. Jessie and Tim—whom I shared my shift with—would understand. Everyone was coming and going for auditions all the time.

I slipped my shoes off and rested my toes against the windshield. When I closed my eyes it was easy to pretend I was at the beach and I felt momentarily grateful for that Los Angeles weather; for the beauty that was everywhere, even when things were terrible.

I thought about texting one of the Joshes, telling him what had happened. Josh K would probably confirm that the struggle was, in fact, real. Josh L would likely respond with a forced intimacy and offer to meet me right there in Koreatown for a cup of tea or something. I didn't want either of these things. I didn't want to seek comfort in either of them.

After work, Maia and I went to a house party in Hollywood, just north of Franklin. The host was a production assistant from the movie Maia was working on, a biopic about a famous female sculptor from the '70s.

"I'm just housesitting," she told us breathlessly. "I mean, obviously." The yard was sprawling and from the hills you could see the lights of the city spread out, a big smear of brightness. We sat beside a pool that tapered into a hot tub, and I dipped my toes into the turquoise half-moon. I knew my morning with Billy was nothing, at most it would register as an annoyance among the people at this party. Just in passing, the woman next to me said a producer was leaving tiny lewd notes folded up between her windshield wipers each day.

We drank cocktails with bitters and gin and slivers of mint that got caught in my teeth. The nights in LA were so cool compared to the Northeast. I missed the humidity, how warm and soft the air could be. I kept checking my phone to see if either of the Joshes had texted, but neither did.

Later, I rested my head against Maia's shoulder in the backseat of someone's Jetta. Her skin was sticky from chlorine. We sped down the canyon, the streets windy and steep, and I closed my eyes, bracing myself for something I couldn't quite name.

MY FATHER'S DEATH IS A LAW SCHOOL GRADUATE

I see her at the airport before she sees me—she alternates between checking her phone and looking around—and I feel a pang of affection or something like pity watching my mother in the wild this way. For the last three years we've only spent time together in controlled settings: my childhood home on the south shore of Long Island or a Chinese restaurant half a mile east on Sunrise Highway.

I've been taller than my mother since I was twelve, and for my whole adolescence I felt long and ungainly, envious of the way she moved her petite body through the world in swift, effortless movements. She was meticulous about her appearance until my father died—her hair was colored every five weeks so not a glimpse of gray could be detected, she'd run a handful of miles on the treadmill in the early morning before school, and she kept a pair of tweezers in the cup holder of the car, plucking out errant eyebrows in traffic. Today her hair is threaded with silver and she is picking absently at the skin around her fingernails. A large navy suitcase sits at her feet and one of those floral quilted tote bags hangs from her shoulder.

"Why did you bring such a huge bag?" I say.

"That's a lovely way to say hello."

"Sorry," I say, "it's just, you're going to have to check it and it's such a pain."

"What difference does it make? And how am I supposed to fit all my clothes into such a tiny little thing?" She gestures to a rounded titanium suitcase that I borrowed from my roommate. We walk toward security and I stare at the maze of people ahead of us in line, slipping off boots and untying sneakers. I'm unnerved by the intimacy of bare feet and fraying socks—the toenails of an older man long and sharp, like claws.

Once we're up in the air my mother opens her purse in the middle seat and takes out an issue of *Educational Leadership* and a Ziploc bag filled with sliced McIntosh apples and baby carrots.

"You look a little pale, honey. Do you feel okay? I have some ibuprofen if you want, or blush?"

"I'm fine," I say. I take off my sneakers. "Also, no one wears blush anymore. And we're about to go be on the beach for four days. And we're on a plane."

"You always want to look your best," she says. "You never know what could happen on this plane. Actually, Laura Stein's daughter met her husband on a flight from Chicago to Newark. It sounds like a romantic comedy but I swear to God it's true. They were seated next to each other and just hit it off." My mother is careful with her words. "Just one of those lucky stories, I guess."

The reality is that I did just start seeing someone. I met Gabe on Tinder about a month ago, but I can't bring myself to tell my mother. Part of my reluctance is rooted in some adolescent need to maintain a sense of privacy (she used to sift through my trashcan when I was a teenager, unfolding receipts and looking for clues about my life like a suspicious, jilted lover), but I've also had so many three-month relationships that I want to hold out a little longer before telling my family, like how people wait to share pregnancy news until the second trimester when the likelihood of miscarriage has diminished.

I plug headphones into the armrest beside me and listen to the blur of static between channels. The man sitting next to me has a shock of red hair and wears a jade ring on his middle finger. He's working on a PowerPoint about earthquakes, dragging 3D boxes toward each other and then away, fault lines sliding in opposite directions so the earth cleaves apart. Three years ago I was getting my PhD in American Studies, but after my father died I took a semester off and haven't gone back. I'm still getting used to the absence of work, that endless reading, which, in its wake, has left a peculiar kind of anxiety. But I felt as though I were suffocating in that beige-colored library carrel day after day, staring at dark, inky prints of American war monuments and documenting their subtle differences. I'd wanted to understand how a political climate affects the ways in which we honor and memorialize our fallen, but it had become too much. Too much death and grieving. I got a few bartending shifts at a cocktail bar in Greenpoint and took an acting class at a studio near Lincoln Center which led to a handful of commercials. *A joke,* my mother assumed—her exact words were, "Is this your idea of a joke?"—but so far I'd been doing okay. Last month I made five thousand dollars as the quirky friend in a yogurt commercial and $1300 as the woman in a tampon commercial who would never again use the store brand option and risk ruining her best friend's engagement party. Generally, though, I got by on tips.

The man next to me closes his laptop and leans back into his seat. I spend seven dollars on three episodes of *Mad Men*, then promptly close my eyes. It will be the first time in years that my mother and I have spent this much time alone together. I was home for a week after the funeral, but there was a constant flurry of rotating family, and my mother and I were each so lost in our own haze of grief that I barely remember us interacting at all. We were more like college students in the same dorm, walking past each other on the way to the bathroom, sipping lukewarm cups of coffee in the kitchen that someone else had brewed. Then my mother won a raffle ticket at a Hadassah fundraiser, and here we are, on our way to Fort Lauderdale for a three-night, four-day, all inclusive, expenses-paid trip.

The only other time we went to Florida was in 1990 to visit my great-aunt and -uncle in Palm Beach and afterward, on an obligatory trip to Disney World. I remember little of the trip, only that I'd insisted on exclusively wearing tie-dyed clothing and that I threw up on the concrete outside the wilted home of the Seven Dwarfs. My father wove his fingers together, caught the vomit in his hands, as if to protect the sacred Disney sidewalk.

Outside the air is thick and steamy, the sky clouded over. Palm trees line the roads of the airport, their crowns wild and feathery. We walk a single block from the airport to the shuttle bus that will take us to the resort.

"Casey, you're still wearing your sweatshirt? It's probably ninety degrees out here."

"I'm comfortable," I say.

"Only a crazy person would be comfortable in a sweatshirt in this heat."

"But *I'm* not hot. Just because you are, doesn't mean we experience heat in the same way."

"Oh, please."

Since my father's death, I've developed this tendency to examine all behavior through what I imagine to be his perspective. An analyst for thirty-five years, what would he say witnessing the interactions between his wife and daughter? Likely he would comment on my attempt to individuate from my mother, to separate. And her need to envelop me. Or, he might even say, to devour me.

I do have my own therapist, Sharon, whom I started seeing when I lived in LA. We've been doing phone sessions since I moved back to New York four years ago, and I've been ambivalent about therapy just as long. Mostly Sharon's like an external hard drive of my brain and can remind me of things that I've willfully forgotten. Like when I'm romanticizing my ex-boyfriend Dean, she'll mention the time he tried to convince me to be poly, or if I'm still obsessing about my cat Sally's death, she'll gently suggest that Sally's a stand-in for my dad and point out that before Sally died she was pissing on my bed daily.

We are outside on the beach, my mother sitting upright on a plastic chair, reading *Educational Leadership* with a yellow highlighter perched between her teeth. She's the principal of a middle school in Nassau County, a position that she has so wholly internalized that when I had slumber parties as a child, she would stand at the threshold of the den, her voice booming, requesting the attention of a dozen of my eleven-year-old friends. She'd remind us that in five minutes we'd all have to file into the bathroom to brush our teeth, and ten minutes later the lights would be turned out.

I'm resting next to my mother on a towel, kneading my chartreuse toenails into the sand as I skim the script for an audition I have next week. I am, as always, reading for the part of the idiosyncratic friend, rolling her eyes and complaining about her job as a librarian as the star laughs over an enormous bowl of salad. (Here my father would say, *How interesting that right after your father dies you decide to switch careers, inhabit a world entirely unlike your own, perhaps a world in which your father is still alive.*)

"Honey," my mother says, "do you think I should get an S.T.D. test?" She says it as though she's been practicing the words in her head. They come out rehearsed and deliberate: Ess-Tee-Dee.

"Excuse me?"

"I mean, that's a thing you and your friends do, right?" Like some trendy drug in high school. *You guys do whippets, right?*

"Yeah, it's not like 'my friends' though. Just any person who's sexually active and responsible."

"I just, you know, your father was the only person I'd ever been with until recently and…"

I am thirty-one and my father has been dead for three years and yet I feel incapable of having this conversation with my mother. On being forced to consider that she has had sex with anybody, let alone a person who is not my father.

"Yeah, I guess you should, then. I mean, it's definitely the smart thing to do."

"But I don't have to get an AIDS test, do I?"

Our familial roles had always been fixed and I understood this was—and had always been—a luxury. I had plenty of friends who grew up being the caretakers in their families, who cooked macaroni and cheese dinners for their little brothers and bathed them while their parents were at work. Gabe's mother was an alcoholic and as a kid he'd regularly wipe vomit from the bathroom floor, feed her Advil and crushed ice when she was hungover.

"You mean an HIV test? I would. I mean, you don't have to. But I do. When I go to the doctor I just ask for one. It's just a blood test like any other."

My mother takes out a can of aerosol sunscreen and sprays the backs of her arms and legs, the scoop of her chest that is exposed above her bathing suit.

"Take some."

"I'm fine," I say.

"You've been getting plenty of color. You should be careful."

"I do have that wedding next weekend and would love to be nice and tan."

"Remind me whose wedding?"

"Aaron and May."

"Oh, right. May's the boy?"

"She's not 'a boy,' Mom. She's a woman. She transitioned, like, four years ago."

"But she still has a you-know-what."

"That's irrelevant."

"A primary sex organ is not irrelevant."

"I can't have this conversation again."

"Oh, please. You always act like I'm so conservative. I'm not *at all*! I understand that gender is a 'social construction,' I think it's so wonderful that things are changing. And plus, I had an abortion, you know."

"L-O-L, Mom. Seriously."

"You're a grownup, Casey! Not one of my students. Can you please not speak in acronyms?"

. . .

I'm feeling restless and wade into the ocean, icy and gray at my feet. It's overcast and the beach is nearly empty except for a lone surfer in a green bodysuit who is dipping in and out of the water, planting his feet firmly and then tipping over. I count to three and then swim out, dunk my head under and do a few breaststrokes before reemerging. It's chilly but beautiful, and as I float on my back, my long hair fanning out behind me, I'm overcome with longing. I wish I were a person who could somehow know that my father was present in the ocean, floating there alongside me in some hazy, unearthly way. I want to be a person who doesn't see the absolute finality of death. Who didn't know with certainty, when my father lay on the ceramic-tiled kitchen floor, after the aneurysm in his brain detonated and burst, that he was gone.

The next morning is bright and cloudless, and we're on a motorboat with our snorkeling instructor, Kyle, holding rubber fins and adjusting our masks. Kyle wears a single seashell on a piece of string around his wrist and makes ocean-related jokes whenever possible (Where do fish keep their money? In a riverbank!). He is handsome in a nineties, *Baywatch* sort of way—with a broad, tanned chest and a dimple in his chin.

"You're adorable," my mother tells him, before easing herself into the water.

I jump in after her and we are just beneath the surface, cloaked in gear, the sun glinting off the water. Beside us is something like a forest of coral, yellow and blue. I take my mother's hand and we follow a school of striped fish—bright and beautiful, impossibly intact.

Later, back on the boat, my mother whispers, "He's so cute, don't you think?"

"He is, but not my type."

And then she says for probably the fifth time on this trip, "I just want you to be happy."

"I appreciate that but I *am* happy. Regardless of whether or not I have a boyfriend."

"Everybody wants to be loved," she says, somewhat sheepishly.

"I'm not disagreeing with you," I tell her and then I mumble something about how being happy and single aren't mutually exclusive. Though I'm mostly arguing on principle because the reality is that being with Gabe has left me light-headed in a way I haven't felt in years. I feel a general sense of calm just knowing he's around, like keeping a tiny orange tablet of Xanax in my pocket, *just in case.*

We sit outside, just before sunset, at a circular bar resembling a tiki hut. My mother wears a black sleeveless top and a denim skirt that falls just above her knees.

"You look pretty," I say.

She smiles. "Look at us," she says. "Two single girls out on the town." With two fingers she drags strands of hair away from my face.

"Very funny," I say.

"I'm not trying to be funny! We're on vacation! Let's go for it. There are so many handsome men here."

"Alright, alright. Take it easy, Mom."

"You think because I'm your mother I can't be a sexual person? Why is it so repugnant for you to think of me as an attractive woman?" Even since she stopped with the excessive grooming and exercise, my mother is beautiful and put together, her face glowing and dusted with freckles, her whole body lean and lithe.

"Why are you trying to provoke me so much? Of course you're attractive. I just don't *want* to think of you as a sexual person. I'm your *child*."

"But you're not *a* child. You're an adult. I just want you to know that I'm not planning to spend the rest of my life alone."

"Of course not. I'm not asking you to do that."

"You are, though, in a sense. You're the only person who hasn't been encouraging me to sign up for Jdate or eHarmony or one of those sites. All of my friends are trying. Aunt Linda's trying, even Grandma."

The bartender approaches and offers a list of specialty cocktails featuring lots of rum and puréed mango and pineapple. I can feel my eyes filling. I ask for a whiskey ginger, and my mother requests something called a *Punky Monkey*.

"Mom, it hasn't been *that* long."

I try to conjure my father's insight; maybe he would note how badly I want to preserve the family structure in which I was raised, how I want to never stop mourning his death.

"It's been three years!" my mother says, raising her fingers.

I fiddle with an orange peel, digging my nails into the foamy white half-moon.

"Do you know what these three years have been like?"

"I'm not trying to compete with you. But Jesus Christ, I lost a father."

Two men sit down beside us. They are dressed in linen pants and Polo shirts. My mother is whispering now, her jaw clenched. "I know that, of course I do."

Once, when I was nine and began to throw a temper

tantrum in a shoe store because all I wanted was a pair of seventy-dollar Doc Martens, my mother grabbed me by the wrist and in a rare physical moment demanded: *You will not make a scene, you will not!*

Now the sun is dipping, and around us the horizon is wide and low, suddenly breathtaking, the sky shifting from pink to violet to blue. We share a plate of grilled calamari and one of the men next to my mother leans over and taps his glass to hers.

"Cheers," he says. "I'm Jerry. This is, amazingly enough, my friend Jerry, too." The man next to him smiles and shrugs his shoulders. "What can you do?"

"Nice to meet you. I'm Sherry, this is my daughter, Casey."

I wait for the lazy joke suggesting we can't possibly be mother and daughter, but it doesn't come.

"Ha, Sherry and Jerry! It's nice to meet you too," one of the Jerrys says. And then the other, who wears a salmon-colored dress shirt, says, "Mind if we skootch a little closer? Have some dinner together?"

The dinner is less unpleasant than I imagined it would be. Jerry One is a public defender outside of Atlanta and Jerry Two is a high school history teacher. They are impressed that my mother was the first female principal in her town. They order another round of drinks and then the four of us split a bottle of rosé. Jerry Two wants to know all the commercials he may have seen me in and I do a little bit where I mimic myself acting, feigning the affected voice of a commercial actress. My mother leans over and kisses my cheek. "My beautiful girl," she says.

I reach down for my purse and feel a wave of alcohol rising in my body. Beneath the bar Jerry One is dragging his fingers against the side of my mother's denim skirt.

She angles her knees toward him so that they brush against his thigh.

I drain the glass and tap it against the bar.

"I think I better get upstairs," I say. "I'm a lightweight and pretty exhausted."

Jerry Two excuses himself as well.

Upstairs, I feed quarters into the vending machine. I buy a chubby container of original Pringles and a pack of Skittles. I sit cross-legged with the snacks in my lap and turn on the television. I think about three years: my father's death is a law school graduate; my father's death is the entire lifespan of my childhood pet rabbit, Ursula; my father's death is the Korean war.

I think of the time when, in ninth grade, my friend Mallory Feldberg's parents went out of town for a weekend, and we were supposed to have a sleepover, but just after I got there, Jason MacBride showed up and Mallory promptly took him to the bedroom and gave him a blowjob (which I would later hear about in minute detail, how Mallory's jaw had ached and how afterward, Jason's semen tasted like ranch dressing in her mouth—a comparison I've not been able to forget).

I set the can of Pringles on the nightstand, too nauseated to eat. My father would ask why the dinner had been so upsetting. Was it an insult to his memory? Or was it because my mother had violated some subtle, unspoken rule about the way mothers and daughters behave in each other's company?

I type out a text to Gabe, *Ugh weird night. You around?* But I don't send it. Gabe's father was in prison on some draconian drug laws for much of his childhood—their interactions were limited to weekly phone calls and twice-yearly visits. I imagine that Gabe will respond and admonish me for being such a brat—tell me that I'm a grownup who has been cared for all my life, that I should want my mother to be happy. *At least you were raised by both your parents. Were allowed to hug them without a fucking guard watching.* But Gabe is too kind to say anything like that, even if he thinks it. I say it to myself, though.

The phone is unfamiliar territory for us but I decide to call him anyway. He picks up after a single ring and the connection is choppy.

"Hi?" I say. "Can you hear me?"

The words are tumbling out and we accidentally talk on top of each other and then pause in the same moments, each of us waiting for the other to respond. I hear a child wailing in the background and the din of an automated female voice, assertive and serene.

"Baby, you're breaking up!" he yells. "I'm on the train, call you later!"

Two hours later my mother comes in, making her way through the hotel room in soft, deliberate steps. She places her purse on top of the dresser and turns off the television, then changes into a nightgown and steps into the bathroom to brush her teeth. She pulls back the comforter and climbs into bed and I pretend to be asleep as she sobs—the sheets gently rising and falling with her labored breath.

I wish I were the kind of person who would gingerly crawl into bed with her, who would ignore my own discomfort, and wrap my arms around her shoulders, brush the hair away from her damp face and say that everything will be fine. Instead, I lie still, my eyes closed, wondering what has made her cry. Perhaps it was just the unfamiliar touch of a man not her husband, but I don't think about it too hard, because on some level I don't want to know. Really what I want more than anything, is for my mother to remain the tiniest bit unknowable.

She's still sleeping when I wake up just before ten. I slide on a pair of flip flops and head to the buffet in the hotel lobby. I load two plates with everything they have; watery eggs and turkey bacon, miniature boxes of Raisin Bran Crunch, a sesame bagel with pats of butter in the center, slices of melon. A mug of coffee for my mother the way she likes it: filled three quarters of the way with decaf, a quarter with regular.

Later, we sit out on the deck, the sky is overcast but still bright. My mother stares down at the piece of cantaloupe as she spears it with her fork.

"You know I actually had a good time," she says. "It's always strange meeting somebody new. But he was kind, I think."

"Good," I say. "I'm glad."

A script is resting in my lap and I ask if she wants to read lines with me. I'm Anna, again, the overlooked best friend, but she can be Olivia, the smug and cheery star, cloaked in running gear, perpetually navigating a love triangle. When I complain about my job, Olivia will encourage me to stand up to my ornery supervisor, because he wouldn't dare fire me. And maybe, as my mother feigns exasperation when two men text Olivia at the same time, demanding her affection, she will see what I see—the chance to embody a life so utterly unlike her own.

HOW TO GET ALONG
WITHOUT ME

These were the things that Gabe told her: when he was eight, he fell from a jungle gym and knocked out his two front teeth (newly grown, a little ungainly, but then they were gone, replaced by small slabs of acrylic, smooth and sleek, the color of milk); in college, he'd drunkenly purchased an alligator from an exotic pet store in a mall in Rockland County and kept it in his bathtub for several weeks until it grew too large and restless; and now, at twenty-seven, Gabe had been sober for nine months. *Eleven, really*, but he'd been smoking weed occasionally during those first weeks, and when he later admitted this to his sponsor, he was kindly told that he'd have to start the count again. She imagined the loss of those weeks, and chips? Coins? She wasn't sure which. How infuriating that must have felt. To have to return something that was rightfully his, something he'd earned. But Gabe didn't seem to mind.

"I feel at peace," he said, "for the first time in a long while." He kissed her then, disarming her with his affection. Twice on the cheeks and then on her mouth, long enough so she could really lean into it, taste the faint flavor of cinnamon on his breath, feel his lips that were both soft and slightly chapped.

This was the beginning, when he was eager and full of charm. She had mostly dated men who were reticent and stony, unwilling to share themselves, and she felt in Gabe something of a kindred spirit. She was constantly, accidentally revealing herself to people. She didn't mean to but the words seemed to spill out of her, like some layer of armor was weathered or missing. She could spend an hour with someone and they would leave knowing about the first time she'd had sex, or that year in high school where she was bulimic, ingesting tubes of Pringles and cartons of ice cream, vomiting it all up before her parents came home from work.

Within just a couple of months, Gabe went from forthcoming to extremely evasive. He would leave town for weeks and if she texted him and asked where he'd gone, his responses were always vague, like *down south*, or *just to visit some friends*. She'd ask him if he could ever just actually answer a question, but he'd shrug his shoulders, smile at her, his eyes two tiny beautiful slits. Whenever he came to her house, he drank water directly from the kitchen sink, dipped his head below the faucet and let it flow straight into his mouth. As if the simple act of opening her cupboard and choosing a glass suggested too much commitment.

Much of the winter passed this way; Gabe would disappear, and she'd feel as though she'd had enough, couldn't take it anymore, but then he'd show up unannounced outside her office and seeing him—the way he leaned against the building reading a magazine he'd folded into thirds—was enough to fill her with something she could easily mistake for love.

One Friday evening there was a blizzard, and the entire transit system shut down for the weekend. They drank warm cider and cooked all the packages of spaghetti she had, then sat cross-legged on her scratchy turquoise rug and ate at the coffee table.

"This feels like a snow day," she said, giving him a kiss.

They played rounds of spit and gin rummy, and had sex beneath her bulky down comforter. And it seemed possible in those tiny moments that their intimacy could last, like it could just stretch out forever. She would use these bits and pieces, the scraps of information that Gabe had shared with her, and she would fill in the spaces on her own. It could be enough, it could be a life together, she thought. She felt a pang of despair when the trains were up and running again.

On a Tuesday night in March, they lay on her couch, the TV on mute, and he told her that when he was a child, his father had been in prison for a long stretch—ten, maybe twelve years. He recalled the six-hour bus rides his family took upstate for just a forty-five-minute visit. And he remembered staring longingly at the vending machine in the corner of the visiting area, taunting him with its shiny Twix bars and bags of Fritos. His father wasn't allowed to hold coins or dollar bills. Some visitors purchased things themselves but this simple fact, that he could spend money and his father could not, felt too unjust to act upon.

For several years, Gabe's father wrote him letters daily, long yellow slices of legal paper filled with small navy print. The pages were textured from the way he'd press so hard against the paper, each word carefully constructed, all in capital letters. Mostly they were directions, instructions for things to do around the house, things that his father would've ordinarily taught him if he had been home. A recipe for meatballs made from ground turkey; how to fix the circuit breaker in the hallway when his mother blew a fuse; the quickest, most direct way to visit Gabe's great aunt who was in a home forty miles west of the city.

When Gabe got older, his father wrote letters trying to teach him how to drive, but it was a difficult, if not impossible, task. How could one convey something like that—describe motions that were so intuitive, so rooted in your body and your sense of space—through the written word. *When your mirror is aligned with the passenger door of the other car, cut the wheel to the left.* His father's tone had begun to sound defeated after that, but Gabe held onto all of the letters, collecting them and keeping them in a plastic three-ring binder.

As he talked, she kissed his face, delicately pressed her lips to his eyelids or his temples. She tried to share some part of herself too, somehow matching his openness. She would've told him anything, but nothing seemed interesting enough.

"I get panic attacks," she said. "And also, I have this vague and chronic feeling that I'm *always* getting away with something. Like some ambiguous and obtuse crime, and one day I'm going to get caught." She told him about the abortion she'd had in college, which was not, in fact, a difficult or painful decision, though she sometimes felt the need to overstate its impact on her. She spoke, briefly, of her own father, who had died not very long before. But her grief felt so uncomplicated compared to Gabe's; her father had been present and loving while he was alive, what was there to even say about it? How much she'd miss sitting on the phone with him while they both watched the news, or periodically opening her mailbox to find newspaper clippings of a band she liked or an exhibit she might find interesting, no letter attached, just a Post-it affixed that said *XO, Dad*. She talked about how her father's death had briefly nudged her toward religion. Not toward God, but to a framework through which to see her grief. She downloaded an app that reminded her to do the Mourner's Kaddish each day during the first year after his death. And still, sometimes she continued the practice at night if she couldn't sleep. Jews were good at grief, she told him. They understood how structure was necessary to get through a day, and that having people bear witness to your suffering could buoy you. And she found that she leaned on her Judaism way longer than the week of shiva or the year of daily prayer.

Gabe smiled at her in a way that was not unkind, but for a moment she wondered if she saw a flicker of disdain in his eyes. That night, they fell asleep without having sex.

In April, he disappeared. They had plans to meet at a movie theater on 2nd Avenue and he simply didn't show up. He didn't call and didn't respond to her text messages (there were five of them, their tones shifting rapidly: *Hey, I'm waiting inside. Everything okay, baby? I'm going home.* Then the next morning: *Really? You're actually not even going to call me, what the fuck is going on?*). Two weeks later, she sent him an email, saying that there were no hard feelings and she just wanted to make sure he was okay. He never wrote back, but sometimes he'd post things on Facebook—a photo of a dog rolling around on some dewy patch of grass, a link to an *Onion* article—so she assumed he was fine.

Over Thai food in the East Village, her friend David said *maybe you just liked the idea of him, you know?* She stared down at her plate, wound noodles around chopsticks. She hated when people said things like this, when they spoke so authoritatively about other people's relationships. As if she hadn't already thought of that, hadn't picked apart each minute aspect of Gabe's behavior, and all their interactions. And yes, she understood that in a way, she hadn't *actually* known him that well, that she had constructed a whole narrative from those small stories he told her. But still she had grown attached to it, to him. For months, each time she got a phone call from a blocked or unavailable number she felt hopeful that it might be Gabe. Sometimes, after she'd gotten a haircut or if she wore a dress she knew he liked (floral, generally, with small iridescent buttons down the front), she would imagine bumping into him on the subway and her eyes would momentarily well up. Mostly she thought of his stories, bound them together in her mind; a book of everything he was willing to offer her.

A year had passed, maybe thirteen months, when she caught a glimpse of Gabe in his car, stopped at a red light on Meeker Avenue. Above him, on the expressway, a trail of trucks sat motionless, their horns blaring in quick, uneven bursts. She crossed the street and noticed him hunched over in his little Honda hatchback. His beard had grown in and he looked tan, impossibly handsome. She felt the loss of him expanding in her stomach and she thought of those letters from his father and she wished that everyone could be as kind and thoughtful as to prepare people for their absences, for the gaping hole that they would leave behind. How nice it would be, if every time you lost someone, they left a manual in their wake. *How to Get Along Without Me*, it would say. It would be filled with tender and pragmatic advice from the old lover, the former best friend, the incisive grandmother. It would brace you for the future, how to manage your solitude, how to fill up all those long, empty spaces without them.

II

PAINKILLERS

When Nina got there, Josh and his law school friends were sitting around the living room playing cards. The TV was on silent and some miniature image of *The Simpsons* was floating around the royal blue screen. Homer was holding Maggie—his arms outstretched—with a look of frenzied panic in his eyes. Josh and his friends were playing a game Nina didn't understand, it seemed that maybe they were making up the rules as they went along. The coffee table was littered with pistachio nuts, and a clamshell that looked like a Japanese folding fan, sat in the center. One of Josh's friends rested a half-smoked joint in its lap.

"Can you scratch me?" Josh asked. "We took painkillers and we're all so itchy."

He was always the same when he was high: distant but receptive to her attention. She kissed his face, along the curves of his jaw bone, and he smiled, a dazed kind of grin.

Later, when they got into bed, Josh was too high to have sex and asked if Nina could scratch his back some more. He took off his shirt and rolled over onto his stomach. This was the most relaxing way to be with him: she was propped up on her side and Josh was basically asleep, his face pressed drowsily into the pillow. He was there, he was hers, and she could be unself-conscious in her affection. He couldn't read anything into her words or that wounded look on her face. She could mouth *I love you* into his back and he'd never know. So she did that and then she dug her tiny, painted nails into his beauty-marked skin.

Earlier that day, at work, she'd gone with a client to a methadone maintenance program in the East Village. Betsy was a middle-aged white woman who looked elderly, with spiky silver hair and a wooden cane, the shaft covered in black and yellow Batman-themed Band-Aids. She was in a court-mandated program, raging war against her heroin addiction. Nina brought her to this clinic, where she would come every morning, take a little sip of methadone and try to get on with her day. It was March and there was a wreath on the clinic door. Tinsel was still hanging sadly around the reception area. Nina felt a brief surge of despair and texted Josh a description of the scene. He responded immediately saying, THE STRUGGLE IS REAL.

Betsy had seemed so tired, but then she saw someone she knew and she raised her cane in excitement. She lifted it up beneath her armpit so that she could hug him.

"Jimmy! Nina, this is my old guy, Jimmy!"

"Be still my heart!" Jimmy said.

Then she went up to the plexiglass window and got her little shot glass of methadone. It looked like cough syrup—thick and orange. When she swallowed, Nina imagined it migrating up into her brain, drenching those wild neurotransmitters, drowning them until at last they were quiet and still, at ease. Afterward, Jimmy and Betsy went to get egg sandwiches at the bodega on Delancey and Nina headed back to the office.

Nina wondered what Betsy would think of her then, in bed with Josh, who would barely call her his girlfriend, who had the most striking green eyes, and who would only let her touch him in public when he was high and itchy from Oxy.

Once, during sex, Josh had removed the condom without saying anything. This was in 2013, before she knew to consider it a grave violation. She responded with a cursory type of displeasure, but there were plenty of ways she could manipulate the action in her mind: *we must be exclusive if he took off the condom* or *he wanted me so badly that he just couldn't tolerate the barrier between us.*

"Baby," Josh said. "Can you scratch a little higher up? A little harder?" Would Betsy be envious or disdainful? Would she think Nina was full of shit or just regard her with pity? Nina had wanted Josh for so many years that it had become impossible to remember why. Maybe she loved him, but she also really didn't like him. Josh passed out and she kept on scratching his back, rough and red, until the skin broke open, just the tiniest bit.

AT FULL CAPACITY

On their third date, Jack and Nina drive to Atlantic City. It's eleven-thirty on a Wednesday night. Earlier in the evening they'd met at a bar in the West Village that masqueraded as a barber shop—complete with upright leather chairs and combs suspended in blue liquid—but the bathroom door opened into a darkened bar with velvet-coated stools and black, textured wallpaper. They had two drinks and then wordlessly got in Jack's car. He turned onto Hudson and it was two seconds too late when Nina realized they were going through the Holland Tunnel.

"Well, fuck, where are you taking me?" she asks.

"We're going to Atlantic City, baby."

"Are you serious? That sounds like a terrible idea."

"That's a silly thing to say. It's just a beautiful sea-town community for families. There's the boardwalk, the Ferris wheel, little kids walking around eating churros and shit."

"And that's why you're taking me there?"

"It'll be fun," Jack says. His voice is calm but he's grinning. "We can gamble a little and then get some rest in a super fancy hotel. We'll drive back in the morning. Plus, how can you resist all that oxygen pumped into the casinos?"

"You're crazy, Atlantic City is a black hole of despair." Nina has never been there and her resistance is mostly an act. She can't tell if Jack is arrogant or reckless or maybe both, but she edges toward him and kisses his face.

Jack plays a couple rounds at the blackjack table while Nina fumbles with slot machines and sips on a vodka soda. She feels a flicker of guilt about calling in sick the next morning. She works in the fundraising department of a homeless services non-profit, but she's not indispensable—someone else can make the same phone calls telling the stories of their *resilient clients*, asking for money so they can continue to provide the *best services possible*.

Jack and Nina go upstairs and he strips the comforter off the bed and they fuck with their clothes still on, just their jeans unzipped and pulled down low. She loves having sex with him like this, like their need is too urgent to take the time to undress. She gets on top and clenches the headboard with her fingers and they both come, quiet and breathless. They turn on the TV and *Sister Act* is on NBC, which they agree is a fun coincidence because of the wild casino scene in the movie.

"We can go right back down there and act it out," Nina says. "Back in the habit!"

She's drifting toward sleep but Jack kisses her shoulder so gently, she holds her breath for a moment. She can't believe she hasn't texted a single person to say she's left the city, but with Jack she feels like if she utters any of it aloud she'll destroy it.

She wakes a couple of hours later, sweaty and disoriented, an infomercial blaring on the television. Someone is advertising knives that can slice a penny in half. Jack isn't there.

She turns on the lights and in the yellow glow of the room she feels fucked. He has driven her ninety minutes out of the city and has left her there. She is a moron for being so easily charmed. It is six in the morning and the sun is just starting to rise, the lights of Atlantic City glittering and sinister. She goes into the bathroom and sits down on the cream-colored toilet seat, pressing the heels of her hands into her forehead. She could just take a bus back to Port Authority, the practicality in and of itself isn't that big a deal, she supposes, but she feels weighed down by the facts; what it means to be left, by Jack, in a hotel room in the middle of New Jersey. Her mouth is so dry she can barely swallow. Then he walks in. He's unsteady on his feet and his eyes are lit up and glassy.

"I couldn't sleep!" he says, "but I won five grand. Breakfast on me!"

A couple of weekends later Nina goes away with her friend Claire from college, to Claire's parents' house in Connecticut: a suburban home with a finished basement and an oblong swimming pool in the backyard.

"He just sounds irresponsible and reckless, or something," Claire says, after hearing about Atlantic City. "But it's kind of hot, I get it."

They're out by the pool and Claire's resting on a float that's supposed to look like a big ice cream sandwich. Nina left her phone in the kitchen so she would stop staring at it, but every so often she goes back inside to use the bathroom or refill a glass of water, and she watches it charging on the ceramic kitchen floor, like a mother checking on her newborn asleep in a bassinet, she thinks. Eventually there's a text from Jack that says, *what are you doing?*

She goes back outside and picks up *Breakfast of Champions*, which she borrowed from Jack's place last week.

"Ah, he underlined something."

"Congrats!" Claire says. "You're dating a regular human who underlines things in books."

Nina flips over onto her back and the float dips down, water rising over her toes.

"Just like, to have any insight into his thoughts feels notable," Nina says. "The idea of him sitting there and feeling moved by a sentence, you know? He's so opaque. It's like a tiny window."

"Into his soul, or something?"

"Don't mock me!"

"Honestly he sounds like another boring privileged white dude to me. He sounds like Josh Kaye. Have you ever noticed you keep dating the same people over and over again?"

"You're kind of being an asshole. Everyone dates the same people over and over again."

"Okay, but I'm just saying, you're like obsessed with this idea of figuring him out, but what if there's nothing to figure out. What if there's no 'there there?'"

They get back to Brooklyn on Sunday night. Nina is subletting a studio in Crown Heights from a cousin who's in South America. There are rusted steel bars on all the windows and a slight slope to the wooden floor-boards, but it's on a beautiful, leafy block, and there are built-in bookshelves in the living room, an ornate non-working fireplace and mantle. She unpacks from the weekend and texts Jack, *you coming over soon? I have to get up early.*

Coming, he says. And then a few minutes later, *actually need you now.*

What's up? she asks.

Outside.

She unlatches the metal lock and the gate scrapes along the concrete. Jack is lying on the sidewalk, his sweatshirt unzipped and spread out beneath him. He's like a child making a snow angel, but he's twenty-nine and it's the end of summer.

"What the fuck? Are you okay?"

"Drunk," he says, pulling Nina toward him. Across the street two terriers circle each other, delicately examining each other's assholes. Their owners, elderly men, are looking over.

Nina kneels down beside Jack.

"Let's get you inside, you little freak."

"I love you," he says. His eyes are closed. "You're my sweet girl. My girl with sweet tits. My sweet tits."

"Okay, okay, come on now. Inside."

"I'm comfy here," he says.

"Impossible." She stands up and reaches for his arms and he follows reluctantly.

Minutes later Jack is asleep on top of her comforter, white cotton with black geometric shapes. His mouth is slackened, his breath smoky from scotch. She kisses his face, presses her lips against the prickliness of his stubble. He is drunk, she knows, so drunk, but still, he said it!

· · ·

Jack's lease is up in the winter and he ends up staying over a few nights in a row and then doesn't leave. Nina's still working at the development office at Healing the Homeless, calling corporate sponsors all day telling them rote redemptive stories about their clients. Jack is working on "projects." He has a bunch of friends who run their own startups and they hire him to develop their website for a few weeks at a time, or he'll respond to a Craigslist ad and for a month he'll do research for a book on 19th-century architecture. But he also gambles a lot. Some days Nina comes home from work and he's hunched over the kitchen table, a dozen browser tabs open on his laptop. He bets on things she didn't even know one could bet on: local elections in random cities across the country, minor league baseball teams in the Pacific Northwest. Sometimes an envelope arrives in the mail from his parents, but they don't discuss it.

One morning he wakes up and decides he wants to join the Army and says he made an appointment at a recruitment office in Midtown. Then he wants to go to med school (this, in spite of the fact that both of his parents are doctors) and enrolls in an online organic chemistry class. For a few days he's amped up and hyper-focused, doing research and talking out logistics with her. *If I started studying now and signed up for the MCATS in April, I could start applying in the fall.* But inevitably the frenzy passes and in its wake is something like depression. It's not that he's irritable or quick to anger, he's just gone; like his body's a motel he can check in and out of for days at a time.

One Sunday afternoon in April they sit beside each other on the couch and Nina makes a Google Doc that they can both access. The idea is that they'll both add to it, writing down ideas about possible jobs or posting links to applications and grad school deadlines.

"It's just so hard being a struggling artist," he says. "Especially when you're not an artist." He laughs at himself, then bites at his cuticles. She cannot quite explain why hearing this fills her with so much affection. She places her computer down on the woven rug beside the couch and climbs on top of him. His fingers are icy against her skin and he cups her breasts, one in each palm, then lifts up her sweater and kisses the skin beneath her nipples.

Later that night Nina goes to the movies at BAM with Claire and her boyfriend Paul.

Jack's out getting drinks with "some buddies" when she gets home. She's in bed by eleven and texts him to say goodnight. But then she wakes at four when he lumbers in. He flips on the light and just stands there with a blank expression on his face.

"Jack, what the fuck?"

His nose is caked in blood and his left eye is swollen shut.

"What happened?"

"Huh?"

Nina gets out of bed and walks to the kitchen. She's pretty sure they have an ice-pack around from when she'd gotten her wisdom teeth out last year. She finds it beneath a Celeste pizza and wraps it in a checkered dish towel. But when she gets back to the room Jack's passed out on the bed. His jeans are spotted with blood and his feet are planted on the floor. She unties his shoelaces—he's wearing black Adidas that look like soccer cleats—and maneuvers his feet out of the sneakers. His socks are damp with sweat and the odor is so pungent she almost gags. She feels something like contempt, blunt and heavy, against her chest.

At work the next morning she writes Jack a carefully constructed email. She tells him she loves him and doesn't want to keep enabling him. She says something has to change. She'll help him find a therapist, get to the root of whatever's going on.

Jack is green on Gchat all day but he doesn't respond to the email. She stares at his name on her chat list for a long time, at the curvature of the letters, their very own miniature skyline.

That night they eat penne with eggplant and ricotta and she places a bottle of cranberry seltzer on the table. Jack's face is cleaned up but his eye is still swollen and rings of purple are beginning to emerge above his cheek.

"What did you mean by 'get to the root?'" he asks. This is classic Jack, to not acknowledge some significant gesture of hers and then casually refer to it later.

"I don't know. Just like, explore where all the drinking is coming from or if you're self-medicating, figure out what it is you're trying to medicate."

"I'm fine, sweet tits, but this eggplant is way overcooked."

They don't talk about her suggestion again for a while, but she spends whole afternoons at work Googling therapists to try to find one that might seem like a good fit. Claire tells Nina to get over her savior complex, because he's never gonna change, and what does he even need to be saved from? But then things seem to be better. Jack has begun volunteering at an animal shelter and brings home fosters on the weekends. He falls in love with a sandy terrier mutt named Bobby and then refers to the two of them—himself and the dog—as The Kennedys. "The Kennedys are going on a walk, do you wanna come?" "The Kennedys are exhausted from the dog run and they're going to nap." Nina finds his unadulterated affection for the dog a bit grating but she is also moved by the simple way Jack cares for him; dutifully walking him four times a day, regularly filling his bowl with Brita filtered water, and brushing his coat absently while watching TV.

"You'll be a good dad," Nina says, as they're falling asleep.

"Especially for one weekend before I bring my baby back to the pet store," he says, adjusting his pillow and turning away.

In the fall, Jack and Nina go on an "eco-friendly trip" to Puerto Rico with Jack's parents, his sister, Zoe, and her wife, Carly. They stay in bungalows by the beach, where the rainwater is recycled, the whole thing is solar powered and resort staff compost the leftovers when guests leave the table.

They eat dinner in a tent shielded from the sun—each night it's a buffet of organic vegetables and grilled fish. Jack keeps rolling his eyes but Nina and Carly marvel at the luxury.

"This is amazing, and very bizarre," Nina whispers, as they're waiting for a fresh pitcher of mint lemonade.

"Get used to it," Carly says. "They take us on vacations like this every year. Zoe keeps complaining about golden handcuffs or whatever, but it beats the one time I went to Niagara Falls with my family when I was seven."

"Same," Nina says and she thinks of the last time she

went on vacation with her family; she and her brother were five and eight, respectively, and the four of them drove from New York to Orlando over the course of four nights. Nina remembers little of the trip except the moment they crossed the threshold into the state of Florida, and she and her brother took off their t-shirts, in gleeful celebration. She texts her brother: *It would've been so fun if M&D had more money! I love vacation. Miss you.*

Back at the table Jack's dad is talking about a new doctor in his department.

"He's brilliant, truly. Did this fellowship at Mass General last year and came up with a new valve-replacement procedure. He's your age! It's wild."

"Wow, Dad," Jack says.

"He must've gone straight from college to med school, which is less and less common these days. These admissions boards want to see that people have really done things, have spent time abroad, volunteered. Maybe Matthew just compressed all that stuff into college summers, who knows."

"Nina, tell us more about what you do," Jack's mother says. She is piercing blackberries with the tines of her fork.

"Tell us what you do is the most boring, American question," Jack says.

"Oh my god, Jack, you're too annoying," Zoe says. "Why are you acting like a sullen teenager?"

"It's okay," Nina says. "I work in the fundraising and development office for an organization that works with homeless people and tries to get them off the streets and into supportive housing."

"Did Jack tell you I do work for Doctors Without Borders?" Jack's dad asks.

"He didn't. That's great. Where do you go?"

"I'm going upstairs for a bit," Jack says. His dad drains vodka and lemonade from his glass and chews on some ice while Nina smiles sheepishly and follows Jack inside. He lies down on top of the white linens, his sneakers resting on the edge of the bed, and closes his eyes.

"He's so self-absorbed. Did you notice how he asked what you did and then he just starts talking over you."

"It's fine, Jack."

"It's not fine."

If you hate him so much, stop depositing his fucking checks, she wants to say.

"Can you not lie down on the bed with your shoes on?" she asks. "It's obnoxious."

The next morning they're out on the beach and the sun is brutal. Nina shifts on her towel to find an angle that's less bright. "You need to be careful, sweet tits," Jack says. "You always think you burn less than you do." They hadn't touched all night, but now he leans over to kiss her. Twice, three times. He plants his palm against her rosy thigh and then they go back upstairs. Jack pours a drop of bourbon into their iced coffees. He lifts her up and places her gently onto the bed, removes her floral bikini bottom and eases her legs apart.

Later, still in the glow of sex, they rent a jet ski and take turns driving, the Atlantic parting and roaring beside them.

The next afternoon they go with Jack's family on a zip-line tour of the rainforest. For two hours a guide leads them, one by one, on suspension cables through the jungle. It's foggy and humid but once they are hoisted up and sailing, there's a magnificent view; the jungle beneath them is lush and green, dotted with pockets of dark, glistening water. Jack squeezes her hand when they are finished. "That was pretty amazing, huh?"

The guide leaves to greet another family and Jack's father says he wants to take a picture.

There is a brief pause. Nina is obviously the most expendable; she knows she should offer to take the photograph, but she does not want to. She wants, in her ridiculous outfit, with her bright yellow hard hat and a harness bisecting her body, to be planted beside Jack, if not forever, in this one, documented moment. She imagines the photograph in Jack's parents' living room, alongside trips to Turkey and Portugal, the British Virgin Islands. And years from now, somebody will ask, *Who's the girl standing next to Jack?* Jack's mom smiles at her politely. And then it's quiet a beat too long, so she cheerfully volunteers.

There are stretches of time—weeks, a month maybe—when Nina feels nothing toward him. She thinks she is done trying to excavate companionship with somebody who offers her so little. She'll feel certain it's over and then, like a generator in the basement of a hospital during a power outage, she'll discover a well of love and desire, and somehow the whole building is aglow—operating at full capacity again.

It's a Saturday afternoon in early March and for three consecutive days it had felt like spring—the sun closer, more radiant. But by now it's winter again. The sky the color of slate, the air dry and cold. They've just finished having sex and it was the kind of sex where Nina knew she could've been anyone, she just happened to be there. Jack's gaze was past her the entire time, staring blankly at the teak headboard.

He's lying on his back, having just pulled out, when he says, "I think I wanna go on tour with Mikey's band."

"What would you do with them?"

"Be their manager or something?"

"I thought that guy Nick was their manager?"

"Well, he quit. Are you trying to make me feel bad?"

"Why would I be trying to make you feel bad?"

"Cause you're embarrassed that I don't have a real job? Or did my dad email you and ask you to put the pressure on?"

"You're being an asshole. I don't care what kind of job you have, I just think you should have one."

The lights are off in the bedroom and it feels like the middle of the night but it's only six-thirty. Nina picks her t-shirt up from the floor and slips it over her head, untangles the pile of jeans and socks and underwear that twisted together. Jack doesn't move. When she turns back to look at him he's on his side, his face illuminated by the dim light of his phone.

"I'm getting sick of this," she continues. "Most people have to get jobs, you know. It doesn't have to be a fucking career you love. Just get a job and you'll stop navel gazing all day."

As she says it, she knows it isn't totally true, but she will never quite figure out how to parse Jack's afflictions. What stems from what, which he has the capacity to change, if any.

"Cool, thanks," he says. "I've never thought about that. I didn't realize you loved capitalism so much. It's not a great look for you."

"Don't... I'm just saying, most people are unhappy when they have that much time to think."

Jack still hasn't looked up from his phone.

"I feel like you're not in this anymore," she says. "Like you're just keeping me around because I'm constantly stroking your ego and doing your laundry."

"I'm *not* keeping you around," he says. "No one's holding you hostage, leave if you want to."

That night she gets ramen with Claire and Paul. She is ashamed to tell Claire what Jack had said, and can easily predict her reaction. *Why are you still doing this,* she'll ask. Nina knows the question will be rooted in affection, but Claire is a person who needs to be adored, who will not stand a partner who feels any ambivalence toward her. Her own shinier brand of pathology, Nina thinks. Instead, Nina tells them an abbreviated version of the story and asks if she can stay over for a couple nights.

"Of course," Claire says, teasing an egg from the broth with chopsticks, "but it's your apartment. Shouldn't he be the one to leave?"

"Yes, but he has the dog... it's just easier for me to leave."

"Honestly, Nina. You really deserve better," Paul says. This is the first time he has asserted an opinion.

"Thank you, that's sweet."

Fuck you, she thinks. *I know you've only gone down on Claire like twice in the last year.*

Staying with Claire and Paul is like being at a charming bed and breakfast. Paul is a graphic designer and everything in their apartment is deliberate and curated. Colorful ceramic vases with succulents line the windowsills and the beds are fitted with violet jersey sheets that are softer than any she's ever owned. The products in the shower are delightful and plentiful—lavender bath salts, an apricot scrub, Aesop shampoo and conditioner.

Nina and Jack meet for coffee a few days later and he brings her two pairs of jeans and a handful of tank tops. They're at a cafe on Vanderbilt Ave where people are dressed in neon running gear. The woman sitting at the table beside them is wearing a shirt that says *Namastay in Bed*. Jack nudges Nina and then groans.

"Do you want to talk about anything?" Nina asks.

"I just finished the new Jon Krakauer book. It was good," he says. "You'd like it."

"Obviously that's not what I meant."

"What do you want me to say, sweet tits?" He smiles and squints at her. "Can I buy you a croissant or something?"

"I would do anything in the world for you to grow the fuck up."

"But would you? That's sort of why you love me, right? You get to be the one who has all her shit together and you get to take care of me, the fuck-up."

"Okay, I'm leaving."

"But you know I'm right. What would you do with all your free time if you weren't trying to fix me?"

"You can stay in the apartment for the rest of the month but then you need to find somewhere to go."

On the way back to Claire and Paul's, Nina thinks of her father after his own father had died. He'd been a good son: changing diapers swollen with urine, bathing him while he stood, stooped over in the shower, his arthritic fingers groping the steel bar in the tub. After her grandfather died, Nina's father expressed relief and sorrow, but mostly there was a hole, he said. So much psychic space he didn't know how to fill.

Nina is busy at work, preparing for a big fundraiser: making arrangements with the floral company and confirming details with the caterers; vegan spring rolls not egg rolls, and a double order of those spinach artichoke pies that had been such a hit last year. She loves this kind of tedious work where the results are so immediate and concrete. The best part is planning the presentation, when participants come to speak about the ways in which their lives have changed, how getting an apartment has allowed them to attain sobriety, reconnect with family, start therapy again. Many of the social workers are jaded by the stories—they know that these successes are just a handful among thousands of homeless people in this city, most of whom are ignored, arrested, sent to jail for falling asleep in a bank vestibule or hopping a turnstile. But Nina has so little interaction with the clients they serve, sitting in a corporate office in Midtown, that whenever she actually meets with them, she is overcome by a renewed sense of purpose. And too, it makes her hate Jack, for all the support he has and how little he appears to appreciate it.

Nina gathers her jean jacket and tote from the coat room at the end of the night and feels for her phone, which is buried at the bottom of her bag, along with loose change and an unwrapped tampon. Zoe has called three times. Jack has been in a biking accident, she says. He will live but there is lots of damage—many broken bones and ligaments, and they're waiting to hear about spinal trauma.

At the hospital, most of Jack's face and limbs are wrapped in gauze. A maze of tubes is draining to and from his body. Blood and saline and painkillers and so many things she cannot name.

"Thank God you're here," Zoe says. "I have no idea why they called me and not you. My parents are on their way. Can you go check on the dog?"

Jack's eyes flutter open and shut. She looks at the golden downy fur on his arms and the dirt that has collected beneath his fingernails.

Bobby is crying and she can hear his nails pawing back and forth against the door. She has never been a dog person, turned off by their indiscriminate affection, but when she opens the door and Bobby hops to her, she begins to weep at the sight of him, so sweet and helpless.

She walks around the apartment, which now feels like a crime scene. She imagines a detective beside her, with latex gloves and a black light, combing through evidence, trying to figure out exactly what Jack had been doing before the accident. His computer is open but dead on the kitchen counter. A copy of *Harper's Magazine* is damp and bloated from a spill. There's a lot of unopened mail. Beside the bed, a piece of gum is stuck to the wall. It's dark pink and dimpled like a raspberry. Nina feels suddenly inert and nauseated and sits down on the floor next to the couch. On the coffee table is *Breakfast of Champions*—the novel that she had imbued with so much meaning.

Later, after that weekend at Claire's, when she asked him about it, he had laughed—*I bought that used, sweet tits, why would I underline random sentences?* Nina never knew if he was kidding, and some frantic part of her wanted to believe that he was. That he was so guarded, he didn't even want her to see the lines that had moved him. She can no longer remember the specific sentences, but also it doesn't matter: she would've read whatever she wanted into them anyway.

USB PORT

Peter wakes up first and texts me, *hi baby, hi boo, hi honey pie*. His residency shifts at the hospital are long: twelve to fourteen hours if he's lucky. I text him periodically throughout the day even though he usually can't respond until the end. (*I'm so tired of begging rich people for money*, I'll say, or I'll send some meme like Mitch McConnell jerking off to a turtle.) Some nights we just sit on video chat and go about our daily routines. I love looking at his face on my little screen, slightly distorted but also revealing; how his facial hair is growing in or how slowly he's nursing the glass of whiskey behind him on the window sill and the big Denis Johnson novel collecting dust on his nightstand.

If Peter isn't working I'll drive down to Philly for the weekend and we'll have some meals and sex and cozy up on the couch and share stories from the week. We have this joke that I'm watching a TV show Peter's producing: "This week on *Stories from the Emergency Room*." He tells me about the teenager who accidentally shot himself in the foot, the bullet square in the middle of his toes. And the elderly woman who's a *frequent flyer* of the ER, who thinks up reasons to call EMS daily because she's lonely.

Somewhere in those thirty-six hours Peter and I have sex again and I drive back to Brooklyn in a giddy haze. For the first leg of the trip I fantasize about moving to Philly. I could have a closet the size of my current bedroom and Peter and I would have a relationship that wasn't defined by coming and going, but regular quotidian things: who would get the Drano from the supermarket? Should we have roast chicken or tortellini for dinner? But by the time I get back to Brooklyn, I feel more grounded and oriented. Peter works constantly and I don't know that I want to uproot my life for him, especially if he won't be around all that much.

We started dating a year ago, when Peter was in his last year of med school in New York and I was working in the fundraising department at a non-profit. Now Peter's doing residency at a hospital in Philly. It's been manageable, but the distance is always in the foreground, like a piece of art that's defined by negative space. Sometimes I tell Peter that I wish our brains had USB ports and I could just plug mine into his and he could upload details about my life that I'm too tired to tell him. *But I don't want to upload it!* he says. He wants the retelling, the intimacy that is born from the very act of sharing. And what I wouldn't give to skip it! To transfer the stories without all the work; all of my thoughts just popping up on his desktop, fully formed.

I'm on the couch with a magazine and my computer resting on my knees. Peter and I are video chatting—though we're not really talking—he's drinking a can of beer and making pasta. My roommate Lily walks in just as I'm tilting the screen to give Peter a little kiss.

Lily and I met on Craigslist and she stays at her boyfriend's place ninety percent of the time, but every so often she's home with groceries and cute little additions to the apartment. Last Tuesday she brought home a stainless-steel bar of soap that removes the smell of garlic from your fingertips, and a rubber colander that connects directly to the edge of the sink.

"Ooh, what'd you get?" I ask her. She gingerly places the packages onto the dining room table.

"Honestly, I can't even remember. I was bored this weekend and got a million things from Etsy." Sometimes I come home from work and the apartment is outfitted in new Etsy decorations: knit cacti or beer koozies that look like pink pussy hats. Today she removes a pillow from an oversized padded envelope. Stitched on the front in block letters it says LOVE IS LOVE.

Look at that sweet little virtue signaling bedding, I text.

It's a cute gesture, he responds. *Just let it be a nice thing.*

Lily catches Peter's face on my monitor and smiles.

"L-O-L," she says, "what are you guys doing? Just pretending you're in a regular relationship? That's cute."

Since the election, Lily has really committed to gestures like these. There's the sign outside our window that says NO HUMAN IS ILLEGAL and a pin she affixed to her puffy coat that says *not my president.* I'm not any better myself. I even stopped shaving my armpits in some futile attempt to *fuck the patriarchy.* My officemate, Danielle, was annoyed. *All these white girls crying about Trump,* she said. *Like this is the first time you realized someone wasn't on your side.* She wasn't wrong.

I set my laptop on the coffee table and look up at Peter periodically; first he's hunched over the kitchen counter reading the news, then changing into sweat-pants, and later clipping his toenails on the edge of his bed. The walls of his apartment are extremely thin and each night at 11:30 we can both hear his neighbor watching *Seinfeld* reruns. Tonight, when we hear the familiar twang of the opening credits, it signals bedtime.

"11:30 already!" I say.

"I should already be asleep," Peter tells me. "Good-night, my love."

In bed, I look at pictures of Peter on my phone, zoom in and out on his face, as though I'm caressing it. Some-times I go on Instagram and scroll back to his earliest posts, mostly pictures of his ex-wife, whom he married just out of college. I wince at a caption that says *luckiest guy on earth* but I keep scrolling. I study the pictures from their wedding; her delicate wrists and unadorned fingernails, and the checkered Vans they both wore with the date and their initials embroidered on the top.

I trace Peter's jaw bone with the pad of my pointer and I think about Lily's comment, a *regular relationship*. She'd meant it in the most benign way, but I wonder if we're only happy because we're apart. If we lived in the same place would Peter constantly compare me to his ex-wife and be disappointed by the ways I couldn't measure up? Would I disdain him the way I did my ex-boyfriend Jack? Repulsed by the smell of his socks or the way he ate smoked salmon straight from the package.

Sometimes New Jersey is an endless stretch of traffic; just highway and gas stations, but on good days I listen to the radio station that only plays '90s hits and I soar down the turnpike, crossing the Ben Franklin bridge in under two hours.

I've just passed the halfway mark when "Always Be My Baby" comes on the radio and it's like I'm shuttled back to sixth grade, dancing in front of my full-length mirror, applying body glitter to my eyelids and around my belly button. In the video, Mariah Carey rocks sensually on a tire swing, a black pond gleaming beneath her. My best friend Heather and I watch and make a list of boys in our grade we would consider kissing.

That year, Heather and I were in honors social studies with Mrs. Jaffe. We liked her a lot; she was young and pretty with thick, inky black hair and a set of bangles that chimed when she moved her hands across the chalkboard. Over Christmas, Mrs. Jaffe and her husband went to Hawaii.

When we came back to school after New Year's, there was a sub in Mrs. Jaffe's classroom. He had a Scottish accent but an eighth grader said he was from Connecticut and trying to sound sophisticated. He stayed for the first three weeks of January and no matter what time of day we had social studies, there was a half-eaten tuna fish sandwich on his desk.

When Mrs. Jaffe came back to school, just after Martin Luther King Day, her hair—still thick and voluminous—had gone completely gray. Mr. Jaffe, we learned, had died in a scuba diving accident in Kauai.

My hips are still shifting around to Mariah Carey when a man in a silver Corolla flashes his brights at me. I glance at the dashboard; the check engine light has been flickering on and off for the last six months, but everything else looks fine. Maybe one of my brake lights is out and he's trying to alert me.

He does it again and then switches lanes so we're parallel and aligned. He is middle-aged in a pale blue Polo shirt with tufts of gray hair and ruddied cheeks. We make eye contact. He motions at me to roll my windows down.

He starts mouthing something that I can't understand and then gestures for me to pull over onto the shoulder. It's midday and there are plenty of other cars around and probably a rest stop a quarter of a mile away, but something hot and knotted blooms in my stomach.

Now this man is trying to communicate with me and I see something frenzied in his eyes, so I speed up and cross two lanes to exit.

I pull into a Dunkin' Donuts lot and turn the volume all the way down so I can concentrate and get my bearings. Across the highway is an old sign for Blockbuster Video—a blue and yellow VHS tape hanging sideways like a broken traffic light. The lot behind it is empty, all gravel and cement, a few patches of grass.

I turn the engine off and take a deep breath. Then the Corolla pulls up beside me. He's about to get out of his car and I lock my doors and lower the window on the passenger side.

"What the fuck. Seriously, what do you want?"

Up close his skin is pocked with acne scars and his eyes are wet behind wire-rimmed frames. I stare at a miniature purple tree that dangles from his rearview mirror and keep my hands braced on the wheel. My jaw, my stomach, each part of my body is clenched, bracing itself.

"I didn't mean to scare you," he says. "But I really, really need someone to talk to."

"Oh," I say, and I feel my insides start to slacken. It seems implausible that this is all he wanted—that this is why he followed me off the turnpike? "I'm sorry," I tell him, "but I just can't do that."

"Okay," he says. "I understand." He just nods and gets back in his car.

I watch his back bumper as he drives away. It's covered with stickers; he boasts that his child is on the honor roll at Freehold Middle School, another is a drawing of green peas, and beneath it, the text: *Visualize Whirled Peas.*

When I walk into Dunkin' Donuts my legs feel strange and unsteady, like I've swerved abruptly to avoid a crush. I order three Munchkins from a teenager behind the counter.

"They're five for two dollars," she says, and fiddles with the hair tie around her wrist.

"That's alright, I'll just have three."

She stares at me. "But they're five for two dollars."

"It's really okay, I'd just like three."

"Are you sure? That doesn't really make sense because if you do the math it's like…"

"Please. Can I please just have three? Please."

When I start to cry she takes a piece of wax paper from a cardboard sleeve, and removes three donut holes from their container on the shelf.

I arrive in Philly an hour later and text Peter to come downstairs and help me find somewhere to park. He bounces down the steps of his row house, wearing running shoes and an old Curious George t-shirt that belonged to his father in the 80s. I climb into the passenger seat and he eases into the car, swiftly adjusting the mirrors and then searching the neighborhood for a spot.

"How was your drive, boo?" Peter is in a good mood ninety percent of the time, even if he's worked a twenty-four hour shift and then has to cook dinner for his widowed father, who lives nearby in Swarthmore. I find this quality equal parts irritating and deeply calming.

"It was fine," I say, and I fidget with the radio.

"So, I'm thinking since we have your car we should drive down to the Italian market and pick up some food for dinner? I'll just hop out for a sec and grab some stuff. Also, Michael and Becca wanted to come say hi later... I told them we might just need a quiet night in but maybe I'd call them after we ate?"

"Yeah, sure, that's fine." We loop around South Street —pass by vintage clothing stores and smoke shops, neon signs advertising vaporizers and their paraphernalia. I want to try to explain what happened, but it feels so anticlimactic that I don't know how to tell it. This is a thing that comes up often in our long-distance relationship; we're constantly narrating our lives to each other and I wonder how much we're losing when we try to distill our days down to anecdotes, how much is just an approximation of intimacy.

Later, after dinner, when we're sitting on his L-shaped couch, drinking a twelve-dollar bottle of wine, when I do actually tell him the story, he exhales loudly, and puts an arm around me.

"I'm so sorry," he says. He sighs again and puts his glass down on a coaster—which is a picture of him and his brothers that one of them made for Christmas. (When I told this to my own brother, he said, *I never understand things like that. Why would I want to put a glass of water on a picture of my face? Or yours, no offense.*) "But, so, he didn't actually touch you or anything, right?" Peter asks.

I stiffen and shake my head and Peter knows he has asked the wrong question. "I mean, that's not the point, but just wondering."

We're silent and then Peter says, "Why do you think he did it?"

"I really have no idea. Maybe he was just lonely."

"But it makes no sense," Peter says, and then he considers various stories; maybe his wife left him, maybe one of his children was in trouble. "It's just very bizarre that he would go so far out of his way, like follow you to the Dunkin', and then just leave."

"Right. Obviously."

"It's such a creepy thing to do," he says. "But there's a weird way in which it's also brave?"

"How is that brave?"

"To just say what you need. To bare yourself to a stranger! So vulnerable."

"That's not how it felt."

"But there's also part of me that wonders if he had some awful fantasy," Peter said. "One he just couldn't follow through on. Isn't there a Mary Gaitskill short story about that?"

"Jesus, can you fucking stop. Can we just talk about something else?" I ask. "Or can we watch something? I didn't want to actually talk about it, I just wanted to tell you. *USB port.*"

"Right, sure. Sorry. What should we watch?"

We spend the next forty-five minutes scrolling through Netflix, then Hulu, then HBO Go. I'm replaying this afternoon's scene in my head; these ambiguous stories have a tendency to get so slippery in my mind. I want to write it all down so it crystallizes, so I can't forget. I open up a note on my cell phone: *silver car, blue shirt, stupid bumper stickers.*

I look over and Peter has fallen asleep, the sleek little remote poised in his palm. *Seinfeld* is playing next door, and George's parents are screaming at each other, their voices shrill and grating. I think about Mrs. Jaffe and the way her body, so explicitly, manifested her psychic pain. How maybe life would be easier if we all wore our afflictions as she had. Is that what Peter was getting at? Was the man in the car doing just that?

Behind us, the dishwasher is running, and if I close my eyes it sounds like a gurgling brook, water lapping at a shore.

CAN YOU PLEASE TELL ME WHAT
THIS IS ACTUALLY ABOUT

When they fight, Nina stops recycling. It's not as though Peter particularly cares about the environment. He takes long showers and drives when it's just as easy to take the train or ride his bike, but she feels a particular satisfaction throwing a can of seltzer away or dumping a pile of newspapers into the trash.

When they fight in the beginning, Peter retreats. He thinks of his parents; how his father once broke a dining room chair because his mother answered the telephone during dinner, and how he had stared at his younger brother and wished they could communicate through blinks, their own kind of Morse code.

If they fight on their way somewhere, Peter walks ahead of her. He is six feet two inches, his strides naturally greater than hers. Usually he slows his pace to walk alongside her, but on these days she hurries to keep up with him, breaking out in a small sweat beneath her bra.

Sometimes when they fight, Nina feels nostalgic for Jack, the last person she dated, when she had felt too uneasy to voice her displeasure and her wounds were hers alone to tend to. He didn't notice the things that Peter does: the dip in her voice when she feels she's been slighted or the way simple things around the house become more effortful—the opening and closing of dresser drawers or the sorting of laundry growing strenuous.

If they fight at night, Peter becomes aroused and wants to harness the aggression into something erotic. Nina consents and removes his clothing—slacks, ribbed athletic socks, a pale blue button-down shirt—but she insists on being on top and will not kiss him.

Some days when they fight, Nina panics. She goes into the bathroom and sits cross-legged on the turquoise bath mat. She exhales slowly, the way she saw in a meditation video on YouTube. She texts her friend Claire, who immediately validates her outrage and says something to the effect of *you're literally perfect, love u so much.*

If they fight on a weekend afternoon, Peter changes into a t-shirt and sweatpants and double knots the laces of his running shoes. He leaves the apartment wordlessly and without his cell phone. An hour passes and Nina begins to worry. She sends him several effusive messages before seeing his phone light up on the kitchen counter.

After a while, when they fight, Nina wants to say: *you know this is an argument you were supposed to have with your ex-wife, right? Because she's the one who left you, not me.* Instead, she runs her tongue along the back of her bottom teeth, against the wire that was fixed in place when her braces were removed two decades ago.

Lately when they fight, Nina says, *can you please tell me what this is actually about?* Because she knows it's not about the restaurant she chose for dinner on Saturday night, or that she forgot to move the car for street cleaning on Tuesday morning and they were fined forty-five dollars. Peter says he's really not interested in being condescended to, but if she's in the mood to infantilize someone, she should call her mom, who really seems to enjoy it.

Often when they fight, she'll try her hardest to cry, but she can't, not since after her breakup with Jack and her therapist prescribed 10mg of Lexapro to "take the edge off." She feels the tension building in her sinuses, but there's no release, just a pressurized stasis. It reminds her of drama class in eighth grade when she learned about *sense memory* and she tried her hardest to conjure up reasons to cry; she imagined her father being hit by a car or her mother getting abducted at the supermarket. She *felt* the sadness but the tears wouldn't come.

. . .

Tonight, after dinner, Nina isn't sure if they're done fighting, but she settles into a long stretch of quiet, and gets lost in an Instagram maze. She is looking at Jack's wife, who mostly takes pictures of lattes with intricate designs; a school of fish, a crescent moon and stars, a trio of hearts. There are some photos of potted plants soaked in sunlight, a selfie in the backseat of a taxi, but Nina is looking for Jack, hoping for the familiar heat of jealousy to eclipse whatever she is feeling for Peter right now; sorrow or preemptive loss, she isn't sure. Later she wipes down the kitchen table where they'd had their take-out. She holds an empty pad Thai container in her hands, poised above the recycling bin, and hesitates.

I DID IT

I'm on the crosstown bus, on my way to work at the Japanese restaurant on Amsterdam Ave. Charlie and his brother are coming for dinner and I can't decide if it's a generous gesture or just a way to get free food. We hit traffic going through the park and the trees are lush and budding all around us. My fifth-grade science teacher once told us there are a hundred and seventy-two species of trees in Central Park, and I don't think I can name a single one. There's so much beauty that I don't know how to classify, that I'm always trying to capture.

My critiques in college photography classes were always the same: *What are you trying to tell us? Why should we care?* These weren't things I knew how to answer. Why did everything need to have meaning behind it?

Behind me on the bus a man is warning his son about the dangers of walking through the park at night, how he should never do it alone, not even as a grownup. I picture myself getting mugged—a man pressing me up against the broad trunk of a tree, demanding that I give up my relationship or my job. I have an instant to decide and I know I'm indispensable to neither.

At Central Park West a woman gets on the bus and smiles as she eases against the cobalt seat beside me. She's holding an oversized tote bag on her lap and a black speckled violin case rests between her feet. Her hair is a fragile halo above her head, white and coiffed.

Six months earlier Charlie and I were in bed doing this thing where we talked about the night we met as though it were years ago, reminiscing about our younger selves, so romantic and reckless. But our relationship had existed only a few weeks then and I know the reminiscing is a way I force intimacy. Carving out some distance for us to say, *Look at this thing we've birthed and tended to, look how it's growing!* We were lying in bed, and I was on my back, holding my breasts together because I can't quite accept the way they have begun to slide, left and right, facing away from each other like some ornery couple in bed.

"Tell me what happened when you first saw me," I say, like a little kid asking to hear the story of her birth. We were wrapped in a blanket the fabric of long underwear, textured and graying. I turned to face him. There were a few hairs sprouting near his jaw and there was something grotesque about them standing there, so sharp and erect.

"You were wearing that dress with the lilies (I'm moved that he can identify what kind of flowers!) and you walked in late, past midnight, and some guy by the door started talking to you, some loser with an upturned mustache."

There is a silken eye mask on Charlie's nightstand, sandwiched in between a pile of books, the elastic band hanging out like a bookmark. I know it belongs to his ex-girlfriend and each time I go to his apartment I'm hoping it'll be gone. I reach out to touch it, but then I stop and try to be *present*. This is a thing I'm working on.

"Keep talking," I say.

"You were coming from the restaurant, I guess? You were in a bad mood."

"I was just tired! I'd been on my feet for like twelve hours."

"Whatever, this dude and his mustache, he was mansplaining all over you, I could just tell you had all these interesting things to say and he wasn't letting you get a word in, and so I came over and…"

"Oh and you rescued me," I say, feigning awe and appreciation. "Otherwise I would've had to like, extricate myself from a conversation like a big girl." Sometimes I hear myself trying to channel a person I want to be. I want to be indignant that he thinks I need rescuing, but I'm not. I *do* want to be saved, I think. I know it's fucked, but I do.

"Hey!" he says. There's a playful lilt in his voice. "It was nice, I was trying to be nice." He kisses me, but it's too early in the morning for tongue and I keep my mouth mostly closed.

"I know how you meant it."

He lowers his head and bites down onto my nipple then takes it in his mouth. When he does this, I can't help but think of him as a baby, latching onto his mother's breast.

"You swept me up," I say, "but then you were still talking to that girl Gemma the whole night. Why'd you ask me to come home with you instead?" This is where he's supposed to say something sweet and trite like, *Because there was just something about you.*

"You really wanna know?" he asks.

There is a trio of succulents on his windowsill, they are small and prickly and I drag the pad of my finger along their spines.

"I really do."

"I've hooked up with Gemma before and she never puts out and I just felt like, I dunno, you'd be more likely."

There is this thing that happens in my body—like releasing the pedal on a trash can and the lid snaps shut —when I'm faced, head on, with the reality of a person. When I realize they're actually in direct opposition to the fantasy I've been nurturing in my head. But I also felt confident that there was something of substance between us. The second time we hung out he admitted to Googling me and finding random photographs from my college literary magazine. And later that night he told me about his father's cancer diagnosis—that he'd been sick on and off for much of Charlie's life. Both of these felt like admissions he wouldn't have made if he weren't interested.

He gives me this big goofy grin. He has a poppy seed wedged between two teeth. "I mean, I'm just being honest," he says. "I'm so glad this ended up being a real thing, but that's like, the genesis of it."

I sit up and twist the plastic rod of the blinds to let some light in. I know he's gonna complain that it's too early for all that sun, but it isn't. It's probably close to eleven. Grow the fuck up, I think.

Instead he says, "Look, I'm trying this thing called radical honesty. I don't want to fake anything with you."

"That's awesome," I say. "You're like, really evolved."

Sometimes I imagine introducing him to my parents. My dad a little hunched over, always with a halved newspaper tucked into his armpit. My mother, in her pale tapered jeans and the sweater she got at Talbots with a forty percent off coupon. Her curly hair is laced with gray and each time she sees me she asks if I think she should color it. I tell her gray hair is cool, to embrace the *golden years* or whatnot. But on this particular night she'd be so thrilled (almost giddy) to meet the guy I'm dating. She'd ask how we met and I'd watch her cheeks pale when I said *He just had a feeling I was easy.*

Somehow months have passed and I'm still working shitty shifts at the restaurant and barely focusing on photography, still doing this mostly on, sometimes off, thing with Charlie. I keep telling my sister that we're about to breakup and sometimes I even lie and say I've tried but he begs me to stay. Julia's in school to become a therapist but even before this she had a habit of trying to find the meaning behind my words. *Why do you think you want to stay?* she'll ask. *You must be getting something out of it.*

The bus is packed and Ninety-sixth Street becomes congested as we approach Broadway. A group of teenagers is huddled outside the McDonald's on the corner, their backpacks heavy and bulging like armor. The older lady beside me inhales and I can feel her ribcage expanding into mine. I watch as she takes out a notebook the size of my palm and stares at its blank pages. She writes in tiny, meticulous script: *I did it!*

I relish the ten minutes before my shift starts; filling up the glass containers with artisanal soy sauce, scooping teaspoons of wasabi from their big plastic tubs and depositing them onto white square plates, squeezing out discs of carrot ginger compote. It's all so methodical and I find solace in its repetition.

It's a Tuesday night and pretty slow. I'm in the back, molding piles of rice onto porcelain dishes when I see Charlie and his brother walk in. Jeremy lives in Chicago but comes to New York often ever since their dad's lymphoma returned earlier in the year. Jeremy's the slightly taller, lankier version of Charlie, with a beard that looks as though it's meticulously trimmed. We make eye contact and Jeremy gives me a wave and then opens his eyes wide like he's just caught me doing something scandalous.

"Lila!" he says and gives me a tight hug.

Charlie rubs his palm against my waist before taking a seat.

"Hey boys." I hand them two laminated menus and tell them they can take their pick of table.

They sit down next to the aquarium and Charlie puffs up his cheeks at the blowfish passing by. I give them tea and water and then bring out appetizers, including dishes they haven't ordered, pork and prawn dumplings, shrimp rolls and some tempura vegetables. When I go back to check on them a few minutes later they're shredding edamame with their teeth—this little bit they do where they're pretending to be cavemen eating vegetables.

"So, how's it going?" Jeremy asks. "How are the applications?"

For the past two-and-a-half years I've been talking about applying to MFA programs in photography. I'm both embarrassed and flattered that Jeremy knows this. That Charlie talks about me when I'm not there feels novel. Sometimes I imagine he's a baby who hasn't quite grasped the concept of object permanence, like once I walk out of the room I assume he forgets I exist.

"They are slowly going," I say. "What about you? How's the world of intellectual property?"

"Fascinating," Jeremy says. "As always."

Charlie works at a startup—one of those companies like TOMS but instead of shoes, when you buy a backpack, a kid in West Africa gets one too. I'm always suspicious of these kinds of projects. Aren't they just plain old capitalism dressed up as something kinder? But maybe that's uncharitable. Maybe the simple fact is that Charlie is helping people and I'm not. And this *is* something I love about him. He isn't so cynical or jaded that he's incapacitated, or so introspective that he's weighed down by a million existential crises. He says he wants to go to graduate school eventually, to study philosophy, but I have a hard time believing it. He's practical and efficient; good at making spreadsheets and talking about *deliverables*.

"How's your visit so far?"

"It's really nice," Jeremy says. "I miss this face, you know?" He slaps Charlie's chin playfully.

"It's an excellent face," I say.

"Our dad's in the middle of a chemo cycle, so it's nice to be here and hang out with him. Lots of quality time during the infusions."

I nod soberly. Charlie has offered little about their dad's condition. Each time I ask he says things seem to be going okay. I know that Charlie vomited the first time he saw his father without hair and that his mom is, what Charlie calls, *manically optimistic* about his condition.

After they finish eating, Jeremy leaves but Charlie stays for the rest of my shift; he sits at the bar and drinks sake, reads the *Times* on his phone. When it's slow he grabs my wrist and I lean toward him for a kiss. These moments of tenderness are infrequent and fleeting, but they're there. Until they dissipate entirely, I can't imagine that I'll leave.

In the cab on the way home, I sit up front because I'm worried I'll get car sick. The driver is gracious and gathers a pile of magazines and an empty take-out container from the passenger seat. We barrel down the West Side Highway and the Hudson is black and gleaming beside us. I can't stop thinking of the woman on the bus and the subtle swell of pride in her face when she closed the notebook and put it back into her bag. Maybe her quiet dedication to the string section paid off and she'd just been offered a solo in the orchestra. Or perhaps after forty-five years of a benign, loveless marriage, she decided to leave her husband. The possibilities were endless, really.

Brooklyn is quiet when we emerge from the tunnel. We move swiftly from one neighborhood to the next; the blocks are open and industrial, then narrow and busy, bodegas punctuating every corner. At a red light, the driver answers his phone, speaking in French. I don't understand much but his tone is loving, soft. *D'accord,* he says. *D'accord, je t'aime aussi.*

I turn to Charlie. In the back seat, he cups his phone in both hands, his face dimly lit, eyes cast downward.

A THIRD PARTY

You and Charlie have been dating on and off for three years when, in September, he moves to Seattle to get a Master's in the Philosophy of Language. He breaks up with you over the phone but later you fly to Seattle and insist he do it in person. The initial conversation went something like this: You were exasperated and said, *What are we doing?* It was meant to be somewhat rhetorical, but then he said, *We're breaking up.* He said it as dispassionately as *We're getting Chinese take-out for dinner* or *We're going bowling tonight.*

He did not ask you to come with him to Seattle. You wouldn't have said yes, but you fantasized often about the conversation. You imagined saying to your friends *I love him so much but I'm not just going to abandon my life here.* Which was true, you weren't. You'd just started working as a librarian at a public elementary school in Kensington. Your family is all here in New York, specifically, most significantly, your older sister, who is having lots of chronic health problems, whom you will not leave. Still, you'd ached for the tug of conflict; to feel at least a little bit torn by the decision.

When Charlie left, the two of you had decided that you would stay together through the first semester and then reevaluate over Christmas. Initially, you liked the freedom and space of long distance. The romance of writing long emails and sending packages of paperbacks and some of Charlie's favorite snacks—hickory smoked almonds and chocolate bars filled with crushed pieces of red pepper—things that he could certainly find in Seattle, but you insisted on mailing anyway. You even bought a vibrator that connected to Wi-Fi so Charlie could control it from his carpeted, two-bedroom apartment near the university. The night of your best friend's thirty-second birthday party, you got drunk on two-and-a-half glasses of the house white and texted Charlie, asked him to turn it to the fastest setting and make you come. He said he was in the library with Brad from his cohort and it would be too distracting.

One thing you noticed about long distance is how quickly you internalized the time difference between New York and Seattle. You'd wake up at eight o'clock and instantly think: *it is 5 a.m., he will be asleep for two-and-a-half more hours*. At night you'd watch episodes of the new *X-Files* and drift off to sleep on the couch, but it was only seven-thirty on the west coast, you couldn't possibly go to bed that early. You always thought you were too selfish to have children and you marveled at the way your mother so effortlessly called her mother "Grandma Esther" and her brother "Uncle Len" just for you. But being with Charlie showed you how easily a mind can shift its contents around, making room for the people you love.

When Charlie broke up with you, in the second week

of October, six weeks after he'd left, you'd just gotten off the bus and were standing on the corner of Flatbush and Park Place. He said *We're breaking up* and you sat down at the closest stoop, one that was splattered with bird shit, like an avian Jackson Pollock. *What do you mean?* you asked. *Are you being serious?* A moment later an ambulance went by and you wondered, absurdly, if it was for you. But the siren wailed and kept on going.

That night, in a flurry of indignant panic, you bought a ticket to Seattle that you could not afford. Then you made a list of things about Charlie that had driven you crazy: that he never voted, not even for Obama's first term, how he said he'd always defer to you about where to go for dinner, as though he were doing you a favor, when really he was just lazy and made you do all the work. And another thing: Charlie applied to six PhD programs and one master's, just in case. You would've understood if he had left you for a doctorate, but for a fucking master's? Everyone knew that was just a money pit, basically a scam.

Do you actually even care about this? you'd asked him. *I can't see it.*

Two days after that phone call and you're on the plane, sitting next to a man who is wheezing softly and you feel calm and confident, maybe even happy. You have always ceded the control to Charlie; you believe there is a kind of power in being open-hearted. And you are certain that when he sees you he will remember everything. How being together feels so easy it's almost like being alone, but better. The day after his father died and he burrowed into you and wept, and you combed his beard with your fingers, in the direction he taught you— following the patterns of his hair; together you poured through the slim, yellowed volumes of poetry in his father's office until you picked one for him to read at the service. There was the trip to New Mexico when you backpacked through the desert and spent the afternoon in the hot springs. You stared at his legs beneath the water, his thighs all taut and muscly. He held onto your fingers and said, closing his eyes against the sun, *does it get any better than this?*

Julia once told you that it was impossible to convince someone to love you, but you think she is wrong; if you try hard enough you just might be able to do it.

At the airport he is waiting for you in a car you've never seen. Watching him, in a gray Nissan Sentra with his hands draped over the wheel, in a city you've never been to before, you feel suddenly like an alien. But then he looks up and you make eye contact and he smiles this big, goofy grin and instantly it is as though nothing has changed, you have not even broken up. He drives north and points out the touristy landmarks: Boeing Field, the stadium where the Seahawks play, the Space Needle. Your nails graze the patch of hairs at the base of his neck and you kiss at all the red lights. He tells you that he FaceTimed with his nephew who just lost his first tooth, and that the tooth fairy is now an insane yuppie who gives out chocolate croissants and hot cocoa, instead of quarters or dollar bills, did you know?

You go visit the house where Kurt Cobain killed himself, the bench beside it where everyone has written love notes and praised his genius. Seattle has more trees than you have ever seen; they are regal and proud, unlike the trees in New York, which always seem a bit unsteady. You could live here, you think. You could be a librarian anywhere. You would call your grandmother every morning and narrate the drive to work, tell her about the lake beside you that is gleaming and placid, how it reminds you of the summer trips you used to take with her to Upstate New York, right below the Catskills. Maybe you'll save a little money on the cost of living and will be able to fly back often.

Charlie's apartment is chilly and smells like artificial vanilla. His roommate is sitting at the kitchen table watching a lecture on his laptop. Charlie does not introduce you. You get into bed and touch each other, but don't kiss. The smell of his body, which is slightly sour, makes you wet because it is so familiar. You climb on top but he squirms and closes his eyes. *We can't,* he says. When you ask why not he tells you that he told his friends he wouldn't. You don't want to be sexist but you think that is something you should've told *your* friends, not the other way around. This breakup is, in fact, a breakup and you do not understand it.

It's just over, he says, not unkindly. *It's run its course. I don't know what else to say.*

You point to all the things that happened recently that contradict this statement. Last Monday he sent you a text that said *I love you, we'll be okay.* Two nights before he left for Seattle he had dinner with your family at a diner on Lexington Avenue and when he left, he said to your father, *See you at Thanksgiving!* Just a few days ago he suggested that the two of you go to Chicago for Christmas to visit his brother's family.

You just want to understand why. If there is some kind of pointed reason he could cite, you think it would make the grief more palatable. You think about the planes that have disappeared mid-flight over the Atlantic, and the families of the victims; they can't rest until they know how it happened. Was it a fire in the engine or some kind of mechanical failure?

Charlie says, *You deserve someone better, someone who's going to appreciate you.*

He is not the first person to say this to you. You don't know how to explain the well of rage it evokes.

Fuck you! Obviously I know that, obviously I want to be with someone who actually wants to be with me.

So then why did you come here? He winces as he says it, like it pains him to ask. Like he has been trying to spare you.

You were taught not to give up without a fight, to hold on to people dearly.

Why did you let me? you ask.

I didn't know how to say no, he says.

You often felt like your relationship with Charlie was a third party, something distinct from either of you, something fundamentally good and precious, that you needed to protect.

Well, I'm sorry I came, you tell him. *I'm so sorry to disturb your academic circle jerk. Were you masturbating to Derrida all day before I got here? What even IS the philosophy of language and who cares? Sorry I have, like, a real job that actually matters.*

See! he explains. *You don't even like me! Why do you even want to be with me?*

In the middle of the night you wake up gagging. You wretch but nothing comes up. You turn on the faucet and sit down on the feathery bathmat and finally let yourself cry: broken, heaving sobs. Your whole body tensing and releasing. It's seven a.m., New York time and you call your sister. *Julia,* you say. *Am I making this up? Did I make up our entire relationship?*

Shh, shh, she says. But you don't know if she is talking to you or telling her boyfriend, beside her in bed, to be quiet.

When Charlie is at class you walk around his bedroom and collect objects you've given him over the years: a book of James Baldwin short stories, a postcard of a cactus lit up with Christmas lights, a Magnetic Fields record that he now uses as an oversized coaster. Things you have not given him: two pairs of plaid boxers wrapped in cellophane, a purple thermos, a vaporizer pen with yellow oil floating in its center. There's also a strip of photographs from your cousin's wedding. You're holding feathered boas and elaborate mustaches but you are both too self-conscious to use them and you're just smiling at each other, your arms weighed down by props. You gather the photograph and the things you have given him and put them in the corner of his room. Like thumbtacks, you hope they will puncture his stoicism.

Later, he comes back in and says, *Oh look, it's like the cemetery of our relationship!*

You go online and see how much it will cost to take a red-eye home that night. There is a two-hundred-dollar processing fee plus the difference between the fares. *Fuck*, you say aloud. *It's so expensive to change the flight.*

Well then, what should we do for the rest of the day? he asks. It is late afternoon. His room faces west and the sun is fiery and pushing against the horizon. *Do you want to see the school? We could go over to campus and get dinner around there. Or maybe grab a drink with Brad and his girlfriend?*

You do not want to do either of these things. His apartment is already imprinted in your brain and you don't want more information, any other scenery to envision how his life here will unfold. The humid dive bar that he'll frequent, where despite his better judgment, he'll kiss an undergrad while waiting in line outside the bathroom. You don't want to see the beautiful, leafy campus with 19th-century stone buildings where he will inevitably linger with a woman after class, pretending he doesn't mind the cigarette smoke, so he can stay and talk to her (probably about some abstract linguistics theory you cannot understand, even if you cared to try, which you don't). You imagine him saying of you, *she was great, a really good person, but she just didn't challenge me intellectually, had no interest in sitting around and shooting the shit about semiotics or whatnot.* Or if he didn't say that, he'd tell her another story, reducing you to a stand-in archetype, an anecdote. Just as his college girlfriend became *the one from Cincinnati, whose mother had M.S.*

You *do* know what it means to study the Philosophy of Language. And later, you will reread old emails from Charlie, searching for signs and clarity, ways you may have misinterpreted the meaning of his words and instead sculpted your own narrative.

You take a shower and wash your hair and feel the tiniest bit revitalized. Or maybe numb and resigned. Together, you take a walk around the neighborhood and go to an Italian restaurant nearby, with a mural of bricks painted along the wall.

A waiter hands you two menus and then scribbles the specials down on the paper tablecloths. When your drinks arrive—yours a vodka soda and his a gin and tonic—you tilt your glass toward his and smile.

The last supper, you say.

Very funny.

But it is, probably.

I'm sure we will have dinner together at some point, one day.

You split a basket of bread while you wait for the food to arrive. You and Charlie slip into easy conversation; the stupidity of the current administration, your father's impending retirement, the hobbies his mother has incurred since widowhood (rock climbing at an indoor gym and updating Wikipedia pages for female politicians).

You are thinking about the last time you had Italian food together, four months ago, the night of the surprise party you threw him. His friends were waiting at a bar two blocks away, and his brother texted you for updates, wanting to know when you were paying the bill, when you were leaving the restaurant, when you were rounding the corner. You remember the moment you and Charlie walked through the door, the scattering of applause and happy birthday cheers. The way you squeezed his hand, so gleeful and complicit.

COMFORT PACK

Lila's older sister was dying. Or rather, she was in hospice. The requirement for which was only that it was possible Julia would die within the next six months. Lila took comfort in this; anyone *could* die within six months.

The social worker explained hospice services to Lila and her parents. He handed them a shoe box called a Comfort Pack, filled with morphine, antipsychotics, and Tylenol suppositories, for when it was too difficult for Julia to swallow. He wore eyeglasses that clasped open and shut across the bridge of his nose. He said it was always possible for six months to become years, sometimes patients just kept on re-enrolling. He said it as though hospice were like a cell phone plan or a gym membership that you could join or cancel at any time.

A tumor the size of a grapefruit was fixed along Julia's spine. Two years earlier, the oncologist had compared it to a kiwi. Rounds of chemo and radiation could not stop its growth, which doctors continued to liken to fruits. Eventually, Lila could not walk through the produce section of a supermarket without having a panic attack. Melons piled on top of each other looked like bombs, raspberries like blood clots.

Lila was about to turn thirty-five and worked as a librarian at an elementary school in Park Slope. She lived in a four-floor walk-up with her boyfriend, Jamie, with whom she was not in love, but who she knew would make a wonderful father. In the mornings before work, when Julia was not yet dying, Lila had lain in bed and browsed Instagram, looking up periodically while Jamie made and packed their lunches. The monotone of talk radio hummed from the kitchen as he wrapped turkey sandwiches in tin foil and poured home-made trail mix into Tupperware containers.

Jamie was a science teacher at the elementary school where Lila worked. Sometimes Lila walked by his class-room and felt her chest swell as he gesticulated wildly to his students and she saw their enthusiasm. They clapped their hands in awe as a volcano of vinegar and baking soda erupted.

When they first started dating, and people asked Lila about Jamie, she remarked that she was drawn to him because he was *good.* Friends commented that Lila's reasoning was rational and unromantic, but goodness was not to be taken lightly. Plus, Julia had liked Jamie from the very beginning. They'd met for the first time, a few months after her diagnosis, when her face was still round and lit, though her hair had already begun thin-ning in patches. (Julia refused to wear scarves or wigs— she had no interest in making her cancer more palatable for others.)

Jamie had moved his hand gently along Lila's back as he spoke to Julia. He neither avoided her illness nor romanticized her bravery. Mostly he asked questions about her recent job as a therapist at a VA hospital downtown. "My father's a vet," he told her, as he loaded lentils onto her plate. "I wish he'd been able to talk to someone like you."

Months later, when Julia's tumor was hovering somewhere between a clementine and a tangerine, Lila had found herself spending long stretches of time fantasizing about the assistant principal. She thought about fucking him while she read *Curious George* aloud to her students and as she unpacked boxes of new chapter books. But she knew she had to repress or ignore these urges, because she could not imagine actually being with someone who did not know or love her sister.

Jamie was from St. Paul and had come to New York several years earlier for graduate school in education. He was 6'3" and had a long, single scar running from his wrist to his elbow, the result of an ice-skating accident when he was seven.

Not long before he'd arrived in New York, his parents had gotten divorced, and since then, he'd dutifully called his mother each night at 9 p.m. Afterward, he practiced science experiments in the living room, facing the quiet glow of Sixth Avenue, depositing pennies in a glass of soda or gummy bears in salt water. When they had sex, Jamie said Lila's name as he was coming, his voice infused with gratitude.

Lila had spent her twenties dating men who only kissed her on the mouth as a precursor to sex, and who told her often—and not unkindly—that they didn't want to "give her the wrong idea." When Jamie appeared, she believed on some gut level that she should be grateful for him. She imagined Julia chiding her for having doubts, despite his clear devotion to her. It reminded her of senior year of high school, when she had only been accepted to her safety school, and decided she hadn't wanted to go to college after all. *You're being crazy*, Julia had said, from the leafy quad of her Ivy League campus, *don't be a snob, it's a perfectly good school.*

Julia was older by three-and-a-half years. She was a senior in high school when Lila was a freshman. A decade passed but Julia still chose the radio station when they were in the car together, picked the restaurants for dinner, and instructed Lila on which flowers to buy for their parents' anniversary. She spoke with conviction about everything: *you definitely need to break up with him, photography MFA programs are a total waste of money, spending two hundred dollars on fall boots is idiotic.* Lila mostly deferred to Julia's suggestions, though she sometimes resented both her sister's certainty and the fact she never seemed to question any of her own decisions.

Julia acted swiftly and decisively throughout her illness; freezing her eggs immediately following the diagnosis and before the first round of chemo, deciding quickly which surgeries to have and which to avoid, and later, when to terminate treatment.

Julia said, "I want to die at home." They were at the hospital on First Avenue, surrounded by walls and curtains that were varying shades of taupe. On the tray beside the bed was a foil container of Jell-O and a plastic pink dome covering soggy lasagna. Lila and her parents winced at Julia's words, so lacking in ambiguity.

"Okay," Lila said, smoothing a packet of Equal between her fingers. "We'll take you home."

Jamie wanted to know how he could help. He arranged for a hospital bed to be delivered to Julia's apartment. He wanted to know what else, but there was not so much to do anymore.

"Have him buy lots of Ensure and Pedialyte," her mother said. "She likes the vanilla Ensure, not the almond. We don't want her to get dehydrated."

"No, Mom," Lila said. "That's not how this works, you don't get it."

It went against every human instinct to stop feeding Julia spoonfuls of yogurt, to not insist upon just one more sip of water, cupping a hand against her chin, so that it wouldn't spill. It seemed impossible to stop. A body needed to be nourished.

Lila thought about the hospitals in Manhattan on September 11th. She had read about the staffs' frenzied attempts to prepare for the survivors coming in, bloodied and covered with soot, gasping for air. They waited and waited, bracing for a chaos that never came.

Lila sat with her sister, waiting for two men from the funeral home to come. Her mother was in the kitchen, on the phone with the rabbi. Her father had been in the bathroom for a very long time.

Lila thought of the way people said *she died and it was like I saw her spirit leave her body.* It did not feel like this to her. Instead, it reminded Lila of when she and Julia were little and shared a bedroom. Lila, picking at stickers that littered her bed frame, going on about the politics of second grade (Anna W took the lizard home over the weekend and nearly killed it! Sophie R cut off all her hair) while Julia drifted toward   sleep,   only   occasionally   murmuring responses. There was comfort just knowing she was there.

Now, Lila kissed each of her sister's fingertips, cool and clammy. She said, repeatedly, as though Julia was worried, "I will be okay."

Jamie had come by the night before, after Julia had stopped eating and drinking. Lila did not want him to be there when it actually happened. But when she watched Jamie say goodbye—stooping to kiss her sister's forehead —she thought, *I will marry him*. No other scenario seemed plausible anymore. Maybe she would still fuck the assistant principal. Or she would send provocative pictures to her ex-boyfriend, Charlie, who seemed entirely indifferent to her since their breakup, but whose father had died from a similar type of sarcoma. Perhaps Jamie would have an emotional affair, over email. She imagined him writing "ever since her sister died, Lila is detached and far away. I love her but I don't feel I have a partner." He would find companionship elsewhere. The woman would sign her email *thinking of you, xoxo*.

But at the supermarket, Jamie would know to head to the produce aisle himself. "Be right back," he'd say, "meet you at the deli counter."

At the funeral, Lila could not stop thinking about having a baby; a newborn to nurse, the delicate weight of a hungry, breathing creature in her arms. She was also preoccupied by a woman in the back, wearing a long floral skirt and Crocs. They were black, but still.

Lila stood next to Jamie and tugged at the sleeve of his suit. She nodded in the direction of this lady—she had no idea who she was—in Crocs. Jamie shrugged his shoulders as if to say, *who cares? We're at your sister's funeral.* Julia would've cared, Lila wanted to say. Julia would've thought it was hilarious. And grotesque. Once, she'd broken up with someone for wearing Tevas on their third date.

These were the things Lila focused on at the funeral. Not her sister's body being lowered into the ground or the clumps of dirt shoveled onto the coffin. She thought about the poor soul who was stupid enough to wear Velcro sandals on a date with her beautiful sister. She thought about fucking the assistant principal. Or Charlie. Or a librarian from the Bay Area she'd met at a conference last summer. And she thought about giving birth, which suddenly seemed very urgent. Like if she did not do it right away, Julia would be inexplicably lost. She felt panic or acid rising from her gut. There was a parkway just outside the cemetery and the whir of traffic was growing louder. Someone was sobbing. The rabbi closed her prayer book gently and said *Amen.*

SO LONG

Thea grinned as she walked toward him, weaving her way through the heavy traffic of Canal Street. Charlie smiled and pretended to look something up on his phone. It was late May but Manhattan felt like a desert that day—blinding sunlight and a dry, brittle kind of heat.

"Charlie!"

"Thea," he said.

They hugged and his arms were loose around her mostly bare back. She stood on her tiptoes and clasped her hands around his neck.

"The sun is brutal," he said. "Let's go inside?"

They walked into a Starbucks and found relief in the cool, industrial air. They stood in line and Charlie stared at the flurry of activity just beyond the window. Two elderly Chinese women crouched beside a blanket covered with bright, geometric-patterned pocketbooks. A trio of men stood beside them on the corner, selling hookahs; tall contraptions with bulbous lanterns and metal piping. They looked like rulers of a miniature, ancient kingdom.

"Can I have something very cold and very sweet?" Thea asked. "Like the peach thing on the poster? Charlie, what do I get for you? Iced coffee?"

He turned toward the counter. "Sure, sure, thanks. Anything cold. I can pay."

They hadn't seen each other in three-and-a-half years. Her hair had always been blond, but today it was nearly platinum, shades lighter than the last time he had seen her, when they both lived in Seattle. Once she'd had a tiny silver stud pierced through her chin, but it was gone, leaving just the faintest scar. She looked inexplicably younger, as if the years away from him had rejuvenated her.

Their drinks arrived and instinctively they sat on the same side of the table.

"Muscle memory," he joked. They were parallel against the cool vinyl bench but Thea turned toward him, just slightly. If someone had taken a photograph and analyzed their body language in a magazine, it would say: *the way she angles her legs toward him, the way her knees graze his, she wants something from him that he isn't willing to offer.* But the tabloid would be wrong, would not appreciate the hidden intricacies of their past.

"It's so good," Thea said, taking a sip of her cold, frothy drink. "You know, there's something so comforting about franchises. That everywhere you go will just have the exact same thing."

"I know you feel that way! Like when we went to Buenos Aires and you insisted we go to P.F. Chang's or Johnny Rockets or whatever."

"I'm a creature of habit!"

"It's pointless to travel if all you want to do is see an Americanized version of the place you're visiting."

"You're a little grumpy these days, huh? Now that you sold your book you have to adopt the trope of the dark, stoic academic?"

"Ha ha."

He looked down at the table, at Thea's hands draped around her drink. She had stopped biting her nails (they were long and oval, painted coral). He wanted to ask if she still picked at her cuticles. He remembered the tiny dots of red that bloomed from her nail beds. Now they were groomed and even and he craved some indication that she was still a little bit tormented, still tortured by the supposed things that kept her from being with him.

"I'm so happy to see you," she said. "So glad."

"You're just here for a few days? For the big day?"

"I am!"

"Just out of curiosity, why'd you feel the need to go to New York just to get married?" He hoped he adequately masked the hostility in his voice. He took a long sip of his coffee and watched the liquid drain from the cup.

"Well, Lucas is here for some shows. He does visuals for these big, ambient noise events. And his parents are here, they live upstate. We just figured, city hall, you know, why not."

"Got it."

"Tell me more about your book. When does it come out?"

"November," he said. "But it's seriously not a big deal. It's a small university press. Probably a total of five philosophy or linguistics students will read it."

"Come on!" Thea slapped his shoulder lightly and he could feel the pressure of her fingers after she pulled her hand away, like sound echoing from a microphone.

"Don't do that," she said. "Don't be so modest, always. It's a big deal."

"Yeah, it's something," he said. "It's not nothing."

Charlie wanted to ask her so many questions. Was she happy? Truly, truly happy with Lucas? Did she ever check out—ignoring his flurry of texts and desperate phone calls, only to reappear later, smiling and affectionate, refusing to acknowledge her absence? Was she difficult and withholding, and then wildly generous with her love? Were her moods still like a metronome, setting the pace of her partner's days? But he didn't want to know the answers, not really.

Thea took another sip of her tea, and Charlie noticed the ring of lipstick she'd left around the straw. He felt a twinge of disgust. How plainly it sat there—the imprint of her lips taunting him. She was so cavalier, leaving traces of herself everywhere.

"So, it's tomorrow, huh?"

"It is!" she said. "We're just going to City Hall, nothing fancy. Did I already say that? Have you ever been there? I've never even been."

"Yeah, it's fine… it's whatever. I mean, we can't have this conversation."

"It's weird," she said. "I mean, obviously it's weird." But still there was a flippant, easy quality to her voice. "I don't want you to think that it's not. That I hadn't, so many times, just assumed it would be you."

"Why would you even say something like that?"

"What?"

"You can't just say that, that you thought 'it would've been us,' and then marry this random dude tomorrow."

"He's not a random dude."

"You throw shit around so casually, like marriage doesn't mean anything, like it could be anyone."

"I didn't say anyone, I just meant that it's complicated and of course I still love you. I thought that was something you'd want to hear."

"Is it cool if I sit here?"

Charlie looked up, heard Thea say *of course* and watched her quickly move their drinks from the center of the table. A teenage girl sat down on the other side of the table. She had a sleepy expression on her face and patches of vitiligo on her wrists, as if a glass of milk had spilled on her arms.

He felt the familiar sting of it: how easy it was, had always been, for Thea to break the fourth wall of their intimacy. Charlie remembered moments of unbearably tender affection—tracing the curves of her ears, kissing the delicate skin above her eyelids. And how effortlessly she could be drawn out of these moments. When a roommate knocked on the door or her phone lit up with a text message.

"I love those headphones," Thea said. They rested around the girl's neck, bright and bulky, the color of green grapes. "Those are awesome."

"Ha, thanks! From *Urban*, if you want them."

"I have to leave soon," Charlie said.

"Seriously?"

"Yeah, I have a meeting with a student uptown at three."

"Your birthday!" Thea said. There was a note of glee in her voice. He could not tell if she was simply happy to be around him, or if it was the fact of her pending marriage. Or perhaps some cruel combination of the two.

"What?" he asked.

"It's 2:12," she said, tapping on the display of her phone. "Your birthday time. February 12th."

"I've really gotta go. See you in another three years, or sooner, or never. Congrats."

They were both living in Seattle when they met. She'd grown up there and he had moved there for graduate school. He'd been homesick and too eager to insert himself into her world. He went to a handful of Mariners games with her father and once smoked a joint with her brother while walking the shoreline of Lake Washington. It was all too premature, he knew, yet their openness had meant something to him. He hadn't been able to turn away from it.

He left Starbucks and walked south and east toward the subway. He felt awash in longing and then shame— they had only dated for eight months, two-and-a-half years ago!

After one stop, the train rose and crossed the East River, the water glittering beneath them. The sky over downtown Brooklyn was darkening; it would rain soon and the heat would break, leaving the sidewalks damp, the air dewy and fragrant. He thought of a Neruda poem he had read in college. He couldn't remember the title, just the one line: *Love is so short, forgetting is so long.* The car lurched forward and a little boy in a fireman's hat dropped a plastic cup. "No!" he cried. "No, no, no no, no!"

Charlie watched as it rolled down the aisle of the train, a trail of crushed iced and orange soda in its wake.

IV

MAKING THINGS UP

It was late January when I started to notice ingrown hairs along my bikini line. Probably two dozen of them blooming around my groin. I showed Becky, who said decisively that they were *not* ingrown hairs. She showed me an actual ingrown hair beside her eyebrow, a black dot aching to break through.

I was twenty-four and working at a literary agency in Midtown. I'd gotten the job through the alumni listserv of the all-women's college Becky and I had gone to, the one where we were awakened each morning by an automated recording telling us we were beautiful, strong, independent women. *We were.*

The agency was on the thirty-second floor of an angular, glassy building. Elevators opened to lots of wide-open space and frosted partitions and the most successful books were encased in shelves that were illuminated by tiny fluorescent bulbs. They were cookbooks with quiet covers (a trio of skewered shrimp, a milky egg and a plate of arugula) and coffee table books about

20th-century sculptors or unlikely friendships between species.

A few days after I found the not-ingrown hairs, I went to an urgent care on Thirty-third Street. I only had an hour for my lunch break and I worried the appointment would take much longer. But I also knew it didn't really matter. Before I'd left the office my boss, Ellen, had asked me to Photoshop the invitation to her daughter's birthday party, an event to which I was not invited. This was before there were websites from which you could download beautifully understated invitations— muted blocks of color or delicate drawings of tulips and champagne bottles.

Outside it was snowing lightly, just enough to make my hair frizzy. I wore too many layers—a turtleneck and a sweater beneath my down jacket—and was sweating heavily by the time I arrived at urgent care.

In the exam room I took off all of my clothes except my bra and a pair of period underwear. The doctor smiled generously. She introduced herself and washed her hands and then examined the bumps.

"Hm," she said. They were raised and pink and slightly dimpled in the center. She took a little booklet from the pocket of her white coat and flipped through it. I stared at my legs; long and dry and unshaven. This went on for a while.

"Ah ha! Just what I thought," she said. "It's a common virus on the playground. My son had it as a toddler. It's also, alas, sexually transmitted." She said it could go away on its own after a couple of months or I could go to a dermatologist to get the bumps frozen off. She referred me to a Dr. K nearby.

I hurried back to the office. The sky was gray and the clouds were heavy and textured; in the distance they looked like mountains. The only person I'd slept with in the last few months was Oliver who worked in the foreign rights department at work. We'd had sex on a handful of occasions, each of which occurred after the assistants went out for happy hour at a summer camp–themed bar on Third Avenue. The first time we'd kissed had been in a forest green rowboat at the back of that bar. A Bryan Adams song had been playing and, indeed, I did feel nostalgic for my actual summer camp. Oliver had red hair, an earnest smile and chronically blushed cheeks. He was excited to be in New York and *humbled by the job*, he said.

"I know it's sort of a cliché," he told me and then described feeling stifled by his suburban Ohio adolescence. "It feels very cool to be here," he continued, "to walk past the Empire State Building every morning. You probably think that's very cheesy."

"I don't," I said. And I didn't. I was envious of this narrative—that his hometown was limiting and that he could attribute whatever unhappiness, dissatisfaction he felt in his life, to his landlocked youth in Youngstown. The squat strip malls and the enormous fireworks store, the parking lots where he and his friends hung out, drinking cans of Pabst. I had grown up in Manhattan within the constant buzzing of the city, taking the subway alone by the time I was eleven, scanning the concert listings in the back of the *Village Voice* at fifteen, going to shows and smoking cigarettes in the back of the old Knitting Factory on Leonard Street. To what could I attribute my angst?

In the truncated rowboat on Third Avenue, I'd told Oliver some version of this and then we'd kissed. His lips were soft and his breath was tangy from beer. We took a cab back to his apartment in the East Village. After we had sex he took two pumps from his inhaler and then went to the kitchen and brought me back a glass of seltzer. He did this each time. It was such a polite gesture it almost seemed like the type of thing his mother had taught him. *Always say please and thank you, hold the door open for your date, offer her a glass of seltzer after you fuck.*

One day in late October, Oliver and I had ended up alone together in the elevator at work. We'd gone all the way up to the thirty-second floor without speaking—or rather, I'd said hi and he'd smiled but he'd mostly looked back down at the fruit he was eating: sliced mango and honeydew in a plastic container. We didn't sleep together after that. Sometimes we'd nod to each other solemnly by the big color printer, which seemed a little dramatic. It was all fine.

But that late January afternoon walking back from the doctor's appointment, I felt anger flickering in my chest. I sat back down at my desk. I had a pile of manuscripts in front of me and was supposed to be reading a novel as a favor to Ellen's next-door neighbor. It centered around an elderly white man making friends with his young Nigerian caretaker. One of the things I had loved about my literature courses in college were how expansive they felt; there was so much room for nuance and interpretation in the texts. My job had somehow turned into the opposite of this, reading was now straightforward and extremely deliberate; yes or no. This manuscript was not good and I didn't have the patience for a tactful critique. "Offensive, tired tropes" I wrote on a sticky pad. Then I texted Oliver, who sat on the other side of the printer and fax machine.

Why didn't you tell me you had an STD?

He responded immediately: *???*

I told him what I had. *I didn't have it before.*

Oh shit! I had that a while ago. Didn't think I still did. So, so sorry.

Dr. K's office was on a fancy block in Midtown, just off Madison Avenue, but in a dreary building with a carpeted lobby and elevators that moved so slowly, it seemed like they resented having to carry people up each floor.

The doctor was on the shorter side and had hair that could be described as spiky. He wasn't exactly handsome but I could tell he thought he was, which made him both more and less attractive to me. His diplomas were framed beside the exam table. He'd gone to medical school in Israel. I wanted to tell him I was Jewish, but I'd never been to Israel, so there wasn't much to say.

"Do you mind showing me the area?" Dr. K asked. I was mostly naked beneath an oversized cotton robe. I moved my underwear from side to side like I did at the nail salon where I sometimes got my bikini waxed. The bumps had spread significantly since my previous appointment and now there were at least two dozen of them down the length of my vaginal lips.

"So here's what we're going to do," he said. "I'm going to freeze these guys off. They're persistent and aggressive, so it's going to take some time. You'll come back every three weeks for a few months. But you're still contagious for the duration of the treatment, so . . ." He removed his gloves and tossed them into a small metal trash can. "Be careful," he said, "or just, know that it's viral and can still spread."

I was vaguely flattered that he thought I would continue to have sex despite this virus growing between my legs. I would not. Frankly, I was relieved to have a concrete reason to take a break from "dating." It was so much easier to hang out with Becky—most nights we fell asleep in the same bed, after smoking a joint and watching DVDs of *The West Wing*. The intimacy between Becky and me was how I imagined lovers felt after decades of marriage. I knew the distinct smell of her gas and at restaurants she could predict exactly what I'd order and which ingredients—eggplant, cilantro, roasted red pepper—I'd ask to omit. Sometimes I felt rageful when she left wet towels around the living room or when I saw her scratching plaque off her teeth while she read. But I also loved her in that way that was fierce and absolute, a way in which I only loved women. I lusted after men and craved their attention, but I never quite admired them or wanted to inhabit their brains like I did with women.

Becky and I had met on a tour the first day of freshman year (*fresh-person,* the guide kept calling us). Becky had lagged behind the rest of the group, conspicuously taking her flip phone out of her pocket, while our tour guide pointed out institutional landmarks. My instinct was to stand up front and respond with the requisite enthusiasm when the tour guide spoke, but I wanted to be more like Becky, to give a little less of a shit about being good or liked.

"You're going to have to remove your underwear," Dr. K said now. I wondered if he thought I was a slut. I didn't really mind either way, but I *did* want to tell him that Oliver and I had used condoms, always, and that I was very careful about safe sex, though clearly it wasn't that kind of STD. "Just so we can make sure to get everything," he said.

He stepped out for a moment while I slid my underwear off. When he walked back in he assembled his tools and put on a pair of latex gloves. He held a container of liquid nitrogen between my legs, as if he were planning to extinguish a small fire.

"So, where'd you go to college? Are you a recent transplant to New York?"

"No, I actually grew up here." I told him where I'd gone to college.

"Ah! My mother *and* sister went there." He seemed genuinely excited. "What'd you study?"

"English, what about you? Or, I guess, you must've been pre-med?"

He swiveled his chair around to get a different angle.

"I was, yeah," he said. "But I wanted to be well rounded. Definitely took an English class here and there."

"Oh that's cool." Just then I flinched; the sensation was so icy it had begun to burn.

"Sorry about that," he said. "Almost finished."

Afterward, he lifted the glasses away from his face and I saw beads of sweat at his hairline. "You can go ahead and get dressed now. Alicia at the front desk will book your next appointment."

At the reception desk I paid the twenty-dollar copay and Dr. K popped his head out from the hallway. "You know what?" he said, "I even took a women's studies class my sophomore year!"

At the second appointment, I ditched the gown and pulled down my pants—gray "trousers" from the Banana Republic Factory on 34th Street—so that the infected area was exposed.

"So what do you do?" Dr. K asked as he washed his hands.

"I work at a literary agency, as an assistant. I read lots of manuscripts, do lots of grunt work, I guess."

"Oh very cool. That seems like a lot of responsibility?"

"Yeah, it can get kinda dark. People spend years writing their guts out and some random twenty-four-year-old reads three sentences and decides their fate."

"Well, it's not random... you got the job for a reason."

"I mean, sort of. Sort of not."

I told him about the fancy celebrity cookbooks and the handful of international literary stars the agency represented, writers from Pakistan and Iran who'd been published for years in their respective countries but were deemed rising stars because they'd been "discov-ered" by readers or critics in the States. I mentioned, too, reading the first chapter of a manuscript and deciding whether or not it was worthy of representation. Our conversation flowed so effortlessly it was easy to forget that Dr. K was burning a virus off my labia.

Becky and I got drinks later that night at a bar around the corner from our apartment. It had a popcorn machine like in an old theater and a projector that showed movies on a wall in the back. That night they played *Edward Scissorhands*. Two guys in jean jackets lingered around us, pretending to fiddle with the popcorn machine. I could tell they just wanted Becky's number. My proximity to her made me both more and less attractive; I'd always be associated with her but also constantly compared to her. I didn't really mind because I agreed with everyone. Becky was beautiful and witty and had perfect breasts.

"So, I think my doctor and I might like each other?" I told her.

"Ew? What?" Becky examined a piece of popcorn.

"We have very good talking-chemistry."

"Hmm," was all Becky said. She had a reserved quality that made me talk constantly; similar to the way I volunteered information to my father precisely because my mother was the parent always asking questions.

Behind us Johnny Depp sat plaintively while Dianne Wiest painted his ravaged skin with different shades of foundation. At the moment it looked lavender. I had seen this movie at least a dozen times—it was one of the only VHS tapes I'd owned as a kid—but I always turned it off before the end. I couldn't stand to see Edward misunderstood, accidentally slicing up Winona Ryder when he was only trying to help.

"I know it sounds sort of… gross? But the conversation is just very organic. And sure, it's a low bar, but he's really good at asking questions," I said.

"Edward Scissorhands?"

"You're annoying," I told her. "The doctor!" This was a thing we discussed often; how guys we went out with were often terrible at asking questions, or didn't seem curious about our lives, that we had to guide the entire conversation, like a docent of etiquette. Becky slept with both men and women, and while the size of her sample was relatively small, she noted this to be a particularly gendered issue. "I hate to be the bearer of boring stereotypical news, but yes, all the women I've dated have been legitimately interested in my life."

Becky had a fellowship at the Mayor's office and a few weeks earlier she'd met a guy who asked what she did for work.

"How much do you know or care about public policy?" she'd asked.

"Very little and very little," he said. We liked that one a lot and often texted it to each other as a shorthand for our lack of interest in a thing—*how was work today? V little and V little.*

That winter I was wearing bulky turquoise headphones in lieu of earmuffs, even when I wasn't listening to music. There was something comforting about the privacy they offered. And even though iPods had been around for a few years, I felt wedded to my Discman, a dark metallic contraption that I carried everywhere. I liked what it suggested about me—that I was committed to the album as an art form, that I took music seriously and didn't just download popular singles off iTunes.

I walked into Dr. K's office that afternoon with the headphones draped around my neck.

"What are you listening to?" he asked me. It was a question I'd always hated for the odd intimacy it revealed. Or rather, I was cautious and deliberate about when to disclose this information. I often resorted to using music as a means to communicate, a shorthand for feelings I didn't otherwise want to articulate. But I tended to wield it in uncool and unsubtle ways, like in eleventh grade when my prom date, Adam, made out with someone else in the bathroom at our post-prom party and I updated my AOL away message with a quote from Elliott Smith's "Somebody That I Used to Know." As I'd hoped, Adam messaged a few minutes later. *Somebody you used to know? Come on.*

I told Dr. K I was listening to a Wolf Parade record.

"Nice," he said. "What album?"

I was surprised that he knew who they were (perhaps because of what his spiky hair suggested to me) and was excited to say that I was listening to their first album, which had come out a couple of years earlier, my favorite.

"Their best one," Dr. K said. And then, as if we were about to sprint onto a football field, "Okay, let's do this!"

Back at work, as I casually walked by Oliver's cubicle on the way to Ellen's office, I wanted him to know that the doctor, a board-certified dermatologist, was intrigued by me. That he asked me questions. That he cared about which album I was listening to and later had asked about my honors thesis on confessional poets. Ellen was on the phone but motioned for me to come in and sit down. She had slender manicured fingers, her nails long and oval, the color of candied apples. She clicked on her mouse impatiently as she waited for somebody on the other end to stop talking. She rolled her eyes in a conspiratorial way and wrote on a chartreuse Post-it: *Grab me some kombucha?*

Our apartment was in Greenpoint, several blocks north of the G train. We each paid five-hundred-and-fifty dollars a month and there were rodents living in our walls. We never saw them but could hear the click of their tiny nails, the way they scurried back and forth beside us. It was early March and felt like the beginning of spring. Becky had invited a couple of people over to have drinks in our courtyard, so I stopped by the liquor store on the corner to pick up a plastic jug of gin and some beer.

Becky's friend from back home, Jackie, had recently moved to Manhattan from Columbus. I didn't like her. Becky said it was because I felt threatened by their history, that she and Jackie had been friends since fifth grade, but I knew it wasn't just that. Jackie had one of those teaching fellowships where over-educated college graduates taught at "inner-city" schools for a couple of years and she fancied herself a Michelle Pfeiffer in *Dangerous Minds.* Our friends Christina and Danny were also there. Danny was our upstairs neighbor and worked for the Obama campaign. He smoked cigarettes in the courtyard constantly—ones that he rolled himself from a little plastic pouch of tobacco.

Obama had just won Super Tuesday and people were having a lot of reductive conversations about race and living in a "post-racial" society, but there was also something thrilling and communal in the air, like the feeling I always got right before Christmas, even though I celebrated Hanukkah.

"I feel really optimistic," Danny said, and took a drag from his cigarette.

"Oh I don't know," Jackie said. "He's what, a two-term senator? Think about everything Hillary's done." I knew she was just parroting something she'd read online.

"It was actually just one term," Becky said. "But whatever. You want me to get started on all the things 'Hillary's done?'" She had just finished plugging in a set of Christmas lights and a long cord was strung through the kitchen window and into an outlet beside the toaster. I felt a little bit in love with her. She was the opposite of Jackie. She read so many outlets and then synthesized her own arguments, nuanced and sturdy. After going to a women's college, there was a tendency among our friends to root unequivocally for Hillary. That Becky didn't—not until years later and then only barely—made me respect her even more. "Let's start with Central America," she said.

Then Becky came over and refilled my mug of gin and sat on my lap. Now I was drunk and felt a rush of affection toward everyone I knew. I wished I could text Dr. K and tell him how much I liked him. How much I appreciated him. How he was so nonjudgmental and professional that I didn't feel ashamed of my warts. I thought of my favorite Wolf Parade song, and I imagined Dr. K reciting the lyrics to me, telling me I was his *favorite thing.*

I even felt moved to text Oliver. *You're just a rly rly good guy.* I typed out. *I know this is weird, because like, who cares, but I just want you to know that I think you're so kind and sweet and I'm not even made at you about the STD.*

"Dude, get off your phone," Becky said. "Who are you even texting?"

"V little and v little," I murmured, and tucked the phone into my pocket.

At my next appointment with Dr. K, I tried to casually mention that I was listening to Handsome Furs, a band that was formed by one of the members of Wolf Parade and his wife. I loved watching clips of them playing together—I could tell how much the husband admired his wife, who hopped up and down while she played on the keyboard. They seemed so happy.

"Oh I haven't heard them," Dr. K said. "Will check them out."

I slid my pants down. It was a Friday and I was allowed to wear jeans to work. Beneath them I was wearing purple nylon underwear. I had wanted to choose something thin and lacy but Becky told me it was bad form; too obvious and also the juxtaposition of the virus against the lace might have the opposite effect of what I was intending.

Dr. K put on gloves and with a small light attached to

his forehead, mined my pubic area for warts. We talked about other bands we liked whose members had dated: Sleater-Kinney, The White Stripes, Yo La Tengo.

"I love them," I said and then immediately regretted it. Who was *them*? Which band was I even talking about. I put my hand over my mouth—an old habit I couldn't shake from when I had braces.

"Things are looking very good," Dr. K said, pressing his gloved fingers across my pubic bone and down toward my labia. "You'll probably only need a couple of more appointments but you're making a lot of progress."

"Oh thanks," I said, feeling a little proud of my resilient body.

Becky had an inviting, gummy smile that made her look sweeter than she really was and later, once I actually knew her, I couldn't believe I'd had the confidence to befriend her. We lived on the same hall in college and sometimes we'd smoke cigarettes together late at night, on the quad right outside the dorms. Becky would tell me about her boyfriend from back home; she and Ethan were in an open relationship, at her urging, which made me feel very provincial. I told her about the boyfriend I'd recently broken up with when he left for school in Michigan, and I feigned a little bit of heartache. Jonah wasn't really my boyfriend, we'd just fucked a few times over the summer because neither of us wanted to go to college without having had sex first.

One night Becky mentioned that she'd joined the pro-choice group on campus and I ended up following her to a meeting the next afternoon. She'd been active in the reproductive rights community in Columbus and had spent afternoons escorting women to abortion clinics, shielding them from protestors shoving photographs of bloody, mangled fetuses in their faces.

"It's so cool you did that in Columbus," I said. "But I don't think that's a thing in New York?"

Becky laughed. "Oh god, you're one of those."

"What?"

"You're in your little bubble and you think everyone around you is progressive and cool. There are anti-abortion people everywhere. I swear there will be people protesting this Midtown clinic."

I was supposed to be the more sophisticated one—having grown up in the city, adjacent to so much wealth, cloaked in privilege by my proximity to so much opportunity. Becky had lived on a cul-de-sac, twenty miles east of Columbus, had graduated high school with the same one hundred kids she'd met in kindergarten. But in a way, this made it easier for her to stand out and create a distinct identity for herself at school. She was the president of the ACLU chapter, led a protest when Walmart moved into town and obliterated the five-and-ten and the local grocery store, and was awarded a state writing prize by the Governor. I was a pretty good student and I liked to read and also stage-managed a few school productions. I wore Free Tibet shirts and went to anti-war rallies here and there, but so did everyone else I knew.

Becky was right, of course, about the clinic. There were only a handful of protestors, but they were there, shouting at total strangers with a hot, blinding rage. I followed her lead and escorted women twenty feet down the sidewalk, ushering them into the building, trying to communicate my solidarity by uttering meaningless assurances.

. . .

At the next appointment, which turned out to be my last with Dr. K, it was unseasonably warm. The sort of day where college students would've been out on the quad, reading in bathing suits or playing frisbee and smoking out of those fake metal bowls disguised as cigarettes.

"Pretty gorgeous outside, huh?" Dr. K asked. I hated that word, "gorgeous." I associated it with retirees in Miami talking about their grandchildren, but it was endearing coming out of his mouth.

"It really is."

"Hey, everything here is looking really great," Dr. K said. "It looks like," he took a breath, "we're all done!"

I was not expecting this and was caught off guard by the prickle of disappointment I felt in my chest.

"Oh wow," I said. "Well, thank you so much for everything."

He took off his gloves in a careful, deliberate manner.

"Any questions or anything else I can help you with?" I wondered if he was trying to prolong the appointment. I pulled up my jeans. They were tight and I had to button them before zipping the fly shut.

I considered making a joke about Botox, but I didn't want to belittle something that was the likely source of most of his livelihood.

"I don't think so?"

"Alright, well. It was great to meet you! Take care, okay? Good luck with those books! Don't be too harsh."

He picked up my chart and headed toward the hallway. Then he paused.

"Who knows," he said, "maybe we'll run into each other at a party or concert sometime!"

"That'd be fun," I said.

I paid Alicia at the front desk and removed one of Dr. K's business cards from a plastic stand beside the monitor. Outside, a homeless man ate a red onion like an apple. He nodded at me soberly and I handed him a five-dollar bill from the back pocket of my jeans.

"Look, it's just kind of weird," Becky said later that night. She was Facebook messaging with a woman she'd met at a salad bar during her lunch break. She constantly met people this way—in line at the movies, reading on a park bench, waiting for the G train. The certainty with which she knew someone was interested in her was baffling to me. I often wondered if I was making things up, culti-vating sexual tension when it wasn't there. Becky was never making things up. On a frigid January day the winter before, I'd been waiting for the light to change on the Upper West Side. I stood at the lip of the street and shivered audibly. Behind me I heard a man's voice: *Oh you cold, baby? Let me warm you right up.* I turned around, already glaring. He was in a green parka, unzipped, wearing a toddler on his chest. *You okay, honey?* He planted a kiss on his baby's forehead. *We're gonna get you home real quick.*

"He's been intimate with your vagina in a way that isn't at all sexy," Becky continued. "And if he does find that sexy, that's even weirder."

"I guess it's like that old Groucho Marx thing. How he didn't want to join a club that would ever have him as a member, or something like that?"

"Exactly," she said and then closed her laptop. "It's just, clearly this dude has boundary issues."

"But maybe I do too!" I was hungry for *something* to happen, wanted to tread the line and linger in that ambiguous space for as long as possible before I knew definitively one way or another.

Becky fell asleep and I went back into my room. I was reading a short story anthology I'd taken from the agency, but I couldn't focus. The rats were clicking their nails above me, rushing back and forth like they were in a relay race. One thing about Becky was that when she slept with people, she did it because she was aroused and moved by some kind of electricity. I was never as present as that and was very deliberate with my choices, thinking of some story I wanted to tell about myself. Once, during our senior year of college, Becky had a threesome with a couple she met at a bar in the West Village. When she told me the story the next morning— how it had all happened so organically, the woman's hand lingering on her thigh underneath the bar, the taxi ride home where they all kissed—I thrummed with envy. It was impossible for me to imagine having a threesome without thinking to myself *I'm having a threesome, I'm having a threesome* on a loop in my brain.

I plugged my headphones into my stereo and listened to the band I'd been telling Dr. K about. I could hear the admiration and also the lust, like a taut cord between the singers. I took off my shirt and held the CD case between my tits. I turned my phone around and snapped a couple of pictures.

At work the next day, I searched the internet for something interesting about Handsome Furs. A tour date or a review echoing what Dr. K and I had already discussed. I found a *Pitchfork* review from the year before that was perfect. I wanted to send him the picture and for him to marvel at how carefree and young I seemed.

Ellen came over to my desk and I minimized the screen.

"I need a favor," she said. "Kylie is extremely,

extremely constipated and nothing is working. Can you try to find me something homeopathic online? I would do it myself, but I have three back-to-back meetings with editors this afternoon." She was trying to close a deal on a debut novel that had gone to auction. The writer was a woman who had grown up in a cult and then found her way to an Ivy League school. I looked up and Oliver was standing at the fax machine, waiting awkwardly for the signal to connect.

I told Ellen I would find whatever she needed.

"Man, that thing takes FOREVER," I said to Oliver. It was the first time we'd spoken since the text about the STD. He looked surprised, but nodded.

"It's the worst," he said.

I spent the rest of the afternoon Googling natural laxatives and reading a dumb manuscript about triplets with magical powers. Just before I left the office, I wrote Dr. K about the band and sent him the picture. I imagined him opening the message, my pale breasts distorted and pixelated on his screen. I felt elated, almost giddy, when I hit send.

When I got downstairs, Oliver was in the lobby. He was hunched over on a marble bench by the elevators. I hesitated, and stared at the enormous neon sculpture in the center of the atrium.

"Are you okay? What's going on?"

He looked up and gestured toward his inhaler. I sat beside him as he took long, deliberate breaths. Eventually I put my hand on his back and rubbed in small, tentative circles. He tensed beneath my touch and it was obvious this act of tenderness was unwelcome. I stood up. I was momentarily queasy with shame, but it dissipated once I thought of Dr. K and the brave picture I'd just sent him.

"I hope you feel better?" I said, and headed toward the revolving door.

Outside, a movie was being filmed. Flood lights decorated the avenue and fake, feathery snow littered the sidewalks. I looked around to try and find the actors, but I saw no one, just a craft services tent and tables filled with sandwiches wrapped in cellophane and little bottles of lemonade.

That night, Becky and Jackie and I went to a party at a loft in Bushwick, which we later learned was infested with bedbugs. I kept refreshing my email, hoping for the thrill of Dr. K's name bolded in my inbox. I drank a Solo cup of watered-down vodka and then turned off my phone and asked Jackie to hold it and not let me look at it for the rest of the night. I didn't want to explain but Jackie just smiled.

"Out of outbox, out of mind," she said.

I hugged her and offered her a sip of my drink.

Months later, after Obama had been elected and before he was officially in office, Becky and I went to a concert at a steamy bar near the Gowanus Canal. From across the venue I saw Dr. K leaning against a wall, awkwardly slurping foam from a plastic cup. His hair looked soft and curly, not spiky at all. He was alone and wearing an ill-fitting button-down shirt. I'd never told Becky I'd sent him that picture and, worse, that he hadn't responded. But I felt cute that night in a short floral dress, boots, and triangular hoop earrings which I rarely wore. I didn't necessarily want to see him, but I wanted him to see me.

I'd recently read an interview with Wolf Parade and learned that my favorite song, "This Heart's On Fire," had actually been written about the lead singer's mother. This was sweeter and more tender than what I'd imagined. Maybe no one ever felt that way about their partner anyway.

While the second band was setting up, I told Becky I was going to the bathroom and handed her my drink. She nodded and took a sip. It had snowed earlier in the day, but the air was sticky and thick inside the bar. I wiped sweat from beneath my ponytail and looped around the venue with my face composed and taut, like when I knew someone was taking a picture of me but I wanted it to seem candid. Just as I was nearing Dr. K, feedback erupted through the speakers, and I saw him cringe and press his fingers to his ears. Then he looked up. He seemed startled but raised his hand tentatively and started to say something. I smiled but kept on walking. The band was struggling; two women were bent over an amp as the drummer sat there idly, holding a drumstick in his mouth. I didn't want to go back to Becky just yet, so I kept walking, weaving my way through the crowd, pretending I had somewhere to go.

SEX ON WEDNESDAYS

It's the first Wednesday in August and Alix has been waiting in line for an hour, standing on the street in Hell's Kitchen, wearing jean cutoffs and flip flops. Her grandmother, Harriet, hated flip flops, which she referred to as thongs. *How can you wear those? I worry someone is going to stamp on your feet, break your little toes!*

Alix can feel the sweat gathering beneath her breasts, imprinting blots of moisture against her tank top. She flips mindlessly between Tinder and Bumble and sometimes Hinge. She isn't even really looking, just swiping left and left and left.

It's nearly 10 a.m. when she reaches the doorway of the studio. Inside, it's dark and cold and seems like construction has been halted midway through; there are rows of metal bleachers and a small stage that is meant to resemble both a home and a doctor's office. There are mauve couches, a plastic exam chair, and some potted plants, but no walls or windows.

Four doctors sit on stage, each with varying degrees of leathery skin, bright teeth, and painted-on eyebrows.

Alix read on Twitter that the lead doctor—Doctor Diamond—a former attending in a level one trauma center in Chicago—sprinkles a handful of authentic Japanese hair onto his head each morning for a luminous effect.

Alix shivers and takes a cardigan from her tote, drapes it across her chest like a smock. Within seconds a production assistant appears beside her, wearing headphones and a tangle of wires at his hip.

"Hey ma'am, do you mind taking that off? You never know when the camera will scan the audience! Thanks so much."

The man sitting beside her smiles tentatively.

"You doing this for the cash too? Or just a big fan of Doctor Diamond?"

"Huge fan. Huge, huge," Alix says.

"Same," he tells her. "I'm Noah."

"Alix," she says, and stuffs the sweater back into her bag. It's a tote her ex-boyfriend Jamie made for her a few months into their relationship—a plain canvas bag he decorated with a Sharpie. In block letters he'd written: *i carry your heart with me (i carry it in my tote).* She has five or six other bags that are hanging on door handles in the apartment, but she can't bring herself to retire this one just yet. It seems to perfectly capture what she loved most about Jamie—how he was silly and soulful and witty at the same time. That he was serious without taking himself seriously.

"This is actually my third time in the audience. Not kidding," Alix says. "You?"

"I don't have health insurance and I'm hoping to just get called on the stage for a physical."

They make eye contact and Alix smiles. She twirls a ring around her middle finger: a tiny, silver cactus.

"I'm just kidding," Noah says. "But also, I *don't* have health insurance and that would be kind of amazing."

"I might be able to help. I actually spend most of my time in doctors' offices these days and I think I've picked up a *lot*. I'm pretty knowledgeable."

"Am I allowed to ask why you spend so much time at doctors' appointments? Or is that like asking how much you weigh or if your parents are paying your rent?"

"Ha. No, it's okay. I'm sort of between jobs at the moment—thus sitting here for an envelope of cash—and hanging with my grandpa a lot. And he's fine but also ninety-three, so we spend a lot of time going to the doctor."

"That's sweet," Noah says.

"It's cool. I like him a lot."

Months earlier, Harriet had died from complications of a fall. This was shortly after Alix and Jamie had broken up and Alix had lost her job at the museum, so she moved into her grandparents' apartment in Queens. Really it was a matter of convenience. But this narrative —that Alix moved in to help care for her grandfather—it was easier for people to digest. It was a nice story. Now she spends her days taking her grandpa, Lou, to doctors' appointments or making money at focus groups (a Visa gift card for $150 after two hours of critiquing a new dating app) or sitting in the studio audience of a talk show hosted by doctors who also want to be celebrities (these pay in cash—crisp twenty-dollar bills for every couple hours).

The studio lights flicker. "Ladies and gentlemen, welcome to *Doctor Diamond*!" The audience erupts in applause. "We're thrilled to have you here, folks. Some housekeeping and then we'll get these brilliant doctors to work their magic! When I raise my hands like this, it means we need some big enthusiastic laughter from you. When I do this it means tons of applause, okay?"

Two hours later, Alix and Noah emerge into the sunlight on the corner of Fifty-first and Ninth and collect their envelopes of cash.

"I want to say let's get a drink," she says. "But that seems kinda untoward since it's not even noon."

"What if we grab some beers and sit on my fire escape instead?"

Noah lives in a railroad apartment in a lonely stretch of Bushwick that's far from both the L and J trains. She follows him through the apartment: the living room strung with chili pepper lights, his roommate's bedroom that's decorated with framed Tom Petty albums and then into Noah's, where a bicycle leans tenuously against the wall and a poster of Nelson Mandela, looking wise and pensive, hangs over his bed.

Outside, the steel of the fire escape is warm against Alix's thighs. She plays with the metal tab of a can of Pabst. The conversation is stiff at first, but after the second beer, they loosen up and trade stories easily. Alix has been on so many dates and job interviews in the last few months that she's perfected her shtick, distilled her narrative down to a few cheeky anecdotes: the grandfather she adores, her parents' fractured marriage (they had both cheated but it was never clear to Alix who had started it, only that it had become a tangled mess of adultery), false starts with her career—a stint in publishing and then in museums. Noah has his too; his parents are first-generation Americans from Greece and worked diligently to provide for their children so that Noah and his siblings could go to college debt-free, and later, when Noah quit his job as a congressional aide to go on tour with his now-defunct band, his parents were dumbfounded and indignant. His sisters, he says, are still on the *right* track, clerking for a federal judge in Connecticut and finishing a PhD in microbiology, respectively. It's easy to mistake all this for intimacy, but Alix knows better.

Noah lights a joint and inhales. He prefers this to a vape pen, he says, the ritual of breaking apart the leaves, rolling the paper and licking the seam shut. He leans over to kiss her and exhales a stream of smoke into her mouth. He tastes like tobacco but she leans closer and there is his deodorant—the same Jamie had worn—just one whiff and her stomach is churning. She climbs on top of him and he carries her inside to the bedroom, dipping his head through the window with his hands cupped around her ass.

Noah removes a single condom from beneath his pillow, which Alix finds vaguely unsettling but not enough to interrupt the flow of things. She's on top of him and thinking *Not Jamie, Not Jamie, Not Jamie* and her mind is now cataloging the people she has slept with who are Not Jamie. She likes to think that each guy she fucks—the accumulation of them—will steadily mitigate the current of loss.

And somehow, five to seven minutes later, she and Noah are both coming, breathless and panting and momentarily disoriented. It's three in the afternoon and she's in a stranger's bed, just a mattress on a box spring, one purple fitted sheet and a single pillow. Having sex with Noah feels both banal and extremely satisfying, like depositing a check at the bank or picking up a sweater from the cleaners.

Heyyyy, Alix texts her friend Becky. *Guess what I did this afternoon?*

Alix is an excellent driver. Her grandfather tells her so each time she drives him to the doctor. There's the urologist, Dr. Grunebaum, every other Tuesday, the optometrist, Dr. Kaplan, most Thursdays, and periodically the cardiologist or the orthopedic surgeon. Never mind that Alix failed her driving test twice—first in college and later, just after graduating—her grandfather wouldn't say it if it weren't true.

This Thursday Dr. Kaplan is out, and the optometrist covering takes his time with Lou. Alix sits in the waiting room, where a Muzak version of an Adele song plays on loop, and she instinctively opens Tinder, barely letting the profiles load before swiping left.

She and Jamie broke up because he decided to go to Thailand, alone, to *learn about himself.* He figured he'd be back in time for the next school year (he'd just finished a graduate program in education) but he couldn't say for sure and he didn't want to feel *tethered* while he was gone. He was the second guy she dated who had left her to travel in Southeast Asia. In a helpless rage, she told him that this was it—if he left there was no chance of them getting back together in the future. But three weeks later, as soon as he left, she began to panic. That he thought of her as rigid and demanding, or worse, needy, made her sweat with shame. *I can be flexible and patient,* she wrote him. Their relationship could surely survive a trip to Thailand. She kept thinking, *If you love something set it free.* She was embarrassed by the comfort she found in the cliché and would be careful not to say this phrase aloud to anyone.

She reached out to Jamie first through email and then texts, which mostly didn't go through. Later, she messaged him on Twitter and then Instagram, as though the various platforms would somehow diminish her desperation, like using multiple credit cards to buy an expensive dress. Three weeks later he responded. He sent her a lovely three-paragraph email detailing his travels; the limestone cliffs beside the Pacific, the electric night markets in Bangkok, and at the bottom: *I think you were right Alix. It's so hard, but I think it was right to be decisive.*

Five months have passed and she's gone on some dates because she knows she should. There was the guy she matched with on three different platforms, a research scientist at a hospital in Midtown, who when they got into bed said "get on your stomach" in a way that was not sexy, only threatening. There was Chris, the classical guitarist with fingernails so long she could feel the scrape when he put a finger inside of her. And then there was Nick, whom she met at a friend's concert. He messaged her on Instagram and asked if she wanted to get a drink. She waited 36 hours to respond and then suggested a dive bar in South Williamsburg, beneath the bridge. He wrote back immediately, *Hey, I think you're SO chill but I actually just started seeing somebody. Take care!*

That was fun, Noah texts her. *Wanna hang again next week?*

Next week sounds far away. But okay, she's not eager.

Def, she responds. *How's next Wednesday?*

That'd be dope, he says.

Lou walks back into the waiting room. He has a goofy smile and uses his cane like he's Fred Astaire.

"Looks like you had fun in there?"

"He dilated my pupils. I feel a little nutty. Take me home?" Alix reaches for Lou's hand. His fingers are bloated and soft, like the paws of a cub, she thinks.

On the ride back to Forest Hills they listen to WQXR and Lou taps his fingers along to Chopin.

"Grandma loved Chopin, you know." It might be true, but he says "Grandma loved this" about every song on the radio, anything they watch on Turner Classic Movies, even a particularly good sandwich he's just had.

"I know, Grandpa."

They drive up First Avenue, where there are still plenty of tenements but also new high rises, glassy and angular, with Walgreens and Starbucks punctuating the corners. On their weekly drives toward the Triborough Bridge, they pass the same landmarks and Lou tells the same stories. He points and says, *That's the corner where I was mugged at eight years old! That's where my neighbor would stand every afternoon during the Depression, selling apples out of a paper bag.*

"You know," Lou says now, "it's okay if you want to get a real job. This seems a little silly, you driving me around all the time. I didn't put your mother through college so that she could have a child who didn't have a real job."

"Alright, alright. Take it easy. I'm happy to be able to spend this time with you."

"What's that?" Lou says, tinkering the hearing aid in his right ear.

"I'm happy to spend the time with you!" Alix says again.

"I know, and you're wonderful. You really are. And I

know it's been a hard time, but Jamie? Really nothing special. And Grandma would want you back at work, not chauffeuring me around like an invalid. She loved bragging about your job."

"Well, sorry, but I was fired, remember?"

"I don't like the word fired."

Alix thinks back to the first week after the breakup, when she lay in bed and watched episodes of *The Office* and took Xanax. She didn't even have the energy (the integrity, her mother had said) to call in sick. Her supervisor called numerous times and some co-workers texted, but the idea of answering seemed impossible. Alix spent the next few days riding different subway lines; she wanted to see how far she could get on a single fare. On the third day she took the 2 from Crown Heights to the 4 at Nevins, up to Yankee Stadium and then the D back downtown, where she transferred to the F at West Fourth, and continued east to Queens. Four boroughs! Riding the trains this way was soothing, like unpeeling a clementine in one long, exquisite ribbon. When she finally showed up at work the following Tuesday, her boss told her kindly that the museum had accepted her absence as a resignation.

"I'm not sure what to tell you, but okay," Alix says. "Also, Jamie was *kinda* special."

"I don't like anyone who doesn't respect and appreciate my grandchildren. He's an idiot. And he owes me twenty dollars."

"Unlikely," Alix says.

Jamie was polite and exceedingly gracious with her family. He always insisted on bringing something to her grandparents' house when they visited, like a bottle of wine or a box of fancy donuts.

"It's true! It was years ago but I swear I lent him some money."

Back at the house, Alix makes dinner—penne sautéed with broccoli and zucchini—while Lou flips between CNN and MSNBC. Donald Trump has officially become the Republican candidate. It all feels a bit like a joke. Alix and Lou agree that there's some relief that it's him, not someone to actually take seriously. Today, he's talking about how much he respects women. How much he wants to help them.

This has become a routine. Lou watches the news and reports back while Alix cooks them dinner. Tonight she clears the table, which seems to be cluttered anew each day with newspapers and napkins, and old ceramic Judaica. Later, they'll switch to episodes of *Curb Your Enthusiasm*, which Lou can't get enough of, and they'll each have two scoops of low-fat Turkey Hill vanilla bean ice cream. It's a grotesque name for ice cream, Alix thinks, but Lou insists it's the only brand he'll eat.

It's Wednesday. The bar in Bushwick has smooth concrete floors and rows of Skee-Ball machines in the back.

"I love Skee-Ball!" Alix exclaims, and she's actually having a good time. "This is totally my kinda sport!"

"Skee-Ball definitely does not count as a type of sport, but that's cute," Noah says. Alix finds a table while Noah orders more drinks. She watches as he leans against the bar and tries to get the bartender's attention. He's handsome, she thinks, and maybe smart, but she wants to *have had* this drink more than she actually wants to experience it, like going to D.C. for the Women's March or getting a graduate degree.

Noah walks toward the table carrying their drinks, nodding his head to a song that Alix can't make out. She offers him a five-dollar bill from her back pocket, but hopes he'll refuse it, which he does.

"I know these dudes!" Noah says, taking a sip of beer. His face is all angles and he has a beautiful head of hair, something Jamie was starting to be self-conscious about. "We did a small tour together a while back."

"Oh whoa, that's cool."

"Honestly," Noah says, "fuck politics and this stupid band. What I really want to do is be a writer."

"Oh nice, I didn't know you wrote."

"Yeah, yeah, I do. In fact, I just wrote this rad short story and a friend of mine thinks I should submit it to *The New Yorker.*"

"Oh, that's awesome. Good for you. I'll be excited to say *I knew you when.*" She drains her gin and tonic in two sips. "Be right back."

In the bathroom, Alix sits down on the closed toilet. She presses *67 and calls Jamie. His phone isn't working in Thailand but sometimes she just likes to hear his voice in the outgoing message. He would've loved Noah's offhand comments about *The New Yorker,* and made a joke about all the white boys who want to be writers, jerking off to *Infinite Jest* or *The Corrections.* Last weekend she downloaded an app that promised to prevent her from drunk dialing Jamie by requiring arithmetic to unlock his number. But even drunk she knows how to disable it, her id determined to get its way.

You've reached Jamie, leave a message.

She stares at the graffiti on the walls: a game of tic tac toe, a few phone numbers, and a stick figure with a thought bubble that says, Trump can suck my WHOLE dick. Alix takes a picture to send to Becky. *In bathroom on 'date' with that Doctor Diamond dude. I'm pretty over it.*

Come hang out with me! Becky responds. *I'm watching a movie. You can sleep over?*

That's very tempting but I also sort of wanna have sex?

Becky and Alix lived together for several years after college, until Alix had left to move in with Jamie. In most ways, Becky is still her home base, the person to whom she feels moored.

That's cool, Becky writes. *Feel free to come over after if it's not too late.*

Noah's roommate is asleep on the living room couch. A screen saver is on the TV, a generic city at sunset, all pastels and glitter. They tiptoe exaggeratedly into the bedroom.

"You're very sexy," Noah says. She rests her tote next to his bed and takes off her clogs, navy and worn. "Can I undress you?"

He removes Alix's jeans and tank top and unhooks her bra, but leaves her underwear on. He puts two fingers into her mouth and then inside of her. He teases her for a while, moving her underwear away, kissing around her bikini line.

"Let's have sex," she says. "Please?"

Noah takes a box of condoms—a package of four—from his nightstand.

"Let me," she says and she climbs on top of him.

It's almost two a.m. when she leaves, too late for Becky. The Lyft back to Queens is forty dollars and spectacular. It's a sparkling clean Camry with packages of Starburst in the backseat and bottled water in a little bucket. The driver is playing *Band on the Run* and they're gliding through Bushwick and Williamsburg, making every light on the way to the BQE. She can't tell if she's happy or sad as she's lulled to sleep by Paul McCartney. *I can't tell you how I feel. My heart is like a wheel. Let me roll it to you.*

A little groggy, she tiptoes into the apartment, which is too warm no matter the time of year. She slips off her clogs and lies down on the living room floor, kneads her knuckles into the beige carpeting. This was the site where her family gathered for every holiday and occasion, somber or celebratory. The kitchen was perpetually stocked to accommodate Alix and each of her cousins, tuna fish with chopped celery and without, orange juice with pulp and strained, skim milk and Lactaid. There's the pink tiled bathroom where she'd gotten her period for the first time, and the long chestnut dining room table where she got tipsy on red wine with her cousins during a seder.

The house, all these years later, even in her grandmother's absence, feels unchanged. Lying on the living room floor, a little drunk, it's as though her childhood's on display, an exhibit she can periodically tour, when she needs to feel the contours, the sturdiness of that familial love.

It's a slow morning, and Lou allows Alix to help him dress, something he rarely does. "The blue button-down," he tells her from the rocking chair beside his bed.

"Grandpa, you have about eleven blue dress shirts. Be more specific."

"Oh, I don't know," he says and waves his hand dismissively. "Just anything, any nice shirt you want. Did

I ever tell you that Dr. Leavitt is second cousins with Ralph Lauren?" He puts the emphasis on the *ren*. "Whose name is actually Ralph Lifshitz?"

"That sounds vaguely familiar."

This is a favorite game among her family members— guessing which celebrities have changed their very Jewish names to something more Anglo. (Her personal favorite is Gene Simmons, born Chaim Witz.)

"Anyway, I can't have Ralph Lau*ren's* cousin thinking I'm a schlub, so please just pick me out a nice shirt, dear."

"This should do it," she says, and displays a turquoise collared shirt.

She guides his arms delicately through the sleeves and then he shuffles to the bathroom, the one place he will not allow her to assist him. He's taking an uncharacteristically long time in there, and she begins to worry that he's fallen, slipped, or something worse. But a few minutes later he emerges, clean shaven, beatific, his shirt drenched with water.

By the next Wednesday, Noah has grown a beard.

"Whoa!" she says, when he opens the door.

"Do you like it?" He rubs his face tentatively.

"I do!" she says. "I totally do."

He pours whiskey and seltzer into two glasses filled with chilled stones instead of ice.

"Classy," she tells him.

Tonight, Alix is wearing a thin black cotton dress with pink flowers. It's her favorite and once belonged to Becky who bought it at a flea market in Chelsea.

"Do you mind?" Alix stands up and removes her underwear.

"Please," he says, smiling. "By all means."

She removes his belt and eases his pants down. She tugs at them when they get stuck around his ankles and then pulls them all the way off.

"I'm gonna climb on top of you now, okay?"

Noah nods.

She kisses him along his stomach and then both sides of his neck. She puts her mouth on his ear, which used to drive Jamie wild. She loved sucking on his earlobes, and the faint, downy fur along his neck.

"Hang on," Noah says. He reaches for the package of condoms on his bedside table. There's only one left. It's fine. Obviously. They aren't exclusive.

She goes through the motions. She moans periodically to try to speed things up. She slaps his ass, presses her palms flat against his balmy skin. She watches his face as he grows closer to coming. His expressions shift rapidly and his eyes open and shut. With his new beard he reminds her of Teen Wolf, a smooth-faced little jock, transforming into a feral creature.

She wasn't going to bring it up but now she can't help herself. She feels nauseous. Nauseated? Jamie was always correcting her.

"So, I just wanted to check in about this. Like, what we're doing—having sex on Wednesdays, I guess? L-O-L. I mean, is there anything we need to talk about? It seems pretty straightforward, I guess."

Noah gingerly removes the condom from his dick and ties it into a knot, like a clown deftly turning balloons into animal shapes.

"Yeah, I mean. I think you're really cool and I really like hanging out."

"Same," she says.

"I just don't like, think about you, when I'm not with you? If that makes sense?"

She nods. It makes sense.

But also, it doesn't. Alix thinks about everything and everyone all the time. Even as she's fucking Noah she's thinking about Jamie, and still, the ex before that from college, who was a tender and generous alcoholic, who'd call her while he was drunk and profess his love to her as he meandered back to his dorm from a party. She thinks of her grandmother, who loved her in the most uncomplicated way, who used to leave her voice messages just saying "You're so wonderful," for no reason at all. She thinks about the Comp Lit course she took in college and the time she got a C+ on a paper and then the professor said that if anyone got below a B on the assignment then maybe they should reconsider whether this school was actually a good fit for them. None of these things preclude her from thinking about Noah, too, who fulfills a particular need in her life right now, and whom she feels slightly repulsed by, but nonetheless wants desperately to want her.

On Friday they see a new internist. Alix drops Lou out front and looks for a parking spot. When she walks into the waiting area he's hunched over a clipboard with his head in his hands.

"What's wrong?"

"I was filling out the paperwork," he says, "and I..."

"What?"

"I can't remember my social security number," he says and breaks into a soft sob.

"Oh, Grandpa. It's okay."

"It isn't," he says.

"I barely even know mine," Alix says.

"It's a very hard thing," he says, wiping his nose with a

used tissue. "You feel like the same person but you're not."

"I'll check Grandma's book at home and I'll call the doctor later and give it to him, okay?"

For decades Harriet kept a spiral-bound purple notebook on the kitchen counter. It was filled with birthdays and phone numbers of everyone in her orbit and she updated it dutifully. She had all three of Alix's addresses from college and the four different apartments in Brooklyn afterward. Alix will go through it later and take stock; she'll be prepared for the next appointment.

"That's not the point, honey."

"I know," she says. "I'm sorry."

The appointment takes a long time. She starts to text Becky, *The most heartbreaking thing just happened.* But then she stops, deletes. She hates the inclination she has to constantly narrate her life to someone.

The waiting room is painted a pale pink and smells like her elementary school cafeteria. She feels a thrum of excitement when the electronic doorbell rings, though she can't say what she's excited for, or who she hopes will walk through the door. She imagines someone she knows walking in—what will they think when they learn she's unemployed and single and living with her grandfather? Will they feel a twinge of pity? And yet it doesn't feel sad today. It feels more meaningful than leading bitchy middle school girls around the museum, guiding them through a simulated tour of a 19th-century tenement, horrified by the way people used to live. The sinks that doubled as bathtubs, the clotheslines that were slung through living rooms, the single beds lined up along the walls in each room, even the kitchen.

. . .

Despite Alix's condom calculations, she and Noah keep fucking. They're rarely in touch throughout the week, but by mid-day on Tuesday they exchange a handful of emojis that generally end with a yellow thumbs up or a check mark. One week Noah tests out cocktails and fixes her a glass of gin and Lillet, Campari and vermouth with a sprig of rosemary. Another night they have sex on the living room couch and then watch two episodes of *Broad City*, while he rests a hand on her bare ankle. She loves the feeling of leaving his apartment, that first rush of air walking out onto the stoop.

"You got home so late last night," Lou says one Thursday morning. He's at the kitchen table, the paper spread out in front of him.

"Did I? I was home around midnight."

"What was that?" Lou reaches into his ear and fumbles with the tiny battery.

"I said I was home around midnight!"

"I'm not asking questions."

"I appreciate that."

"But your mother is curious these days—she wants to know what you're doing. She'd be very happy to know you're dating."

The word *dating* makes her feel slightly queasy—incongruous with what's actually happening—or what her family would imagine. That they envision her being courted in some old-fashioned way, Noah buying her dinner and gently kissing her on the lips before hailing her a taxi, fills her with a sort of shame.

Alix puts two pieces of rye bread into the toaster and joins Lou at the table.

"Dating's pretty different these days."

"Everything's different," Lou says. "You walk around with your face glued to a machine. You think I don't know?"

"Sure, but I just mean, like, people don't 'date' the way you imagine it. And you and Grandma were so young when you met, you weren't even fully formed humans when you committed to each other."

"What's that supposed to mean?"

"I don't know, I feel like the internet makes it simultaneously easier and harder to meet people. But that's not even it, really. I just miss Jamie. And the idea of starting over feels so sad and impossible."

Lou lets out an icy laugh and takes a sip of coffee.

"What?"

"Alix."

"Yes?"

"I was married to Grandma for sixty-six years."

"I know."

"You think I don't know what it feels like to miss someone? I've barely had dinner without her since goddamn Eisenhower was president."

"I'm sorry," she says. "Of course, I know you do."

"This was a good idea your mother had… you driving me to appointments and making me dinner. It's nice, it is."

"Okay? And?"

"And you get something out of this too."

Lou moves from his chair carefully, pressing his hands on the table for support and then pulls his walker closer. He pours his coffee into the sink.

"Don't waste your toast," he says.

. . .

Alix uses Lou's membership to the Forest Hills Jewish Center and goes swimming. She is practicing *self-care*. She swims some laps and thinks *only a person who has their shit together swims laps.* A group of orthodox women swim in long t-shirts over their bathing suits. They shower in the shirts, too, and stare at Alix's naked body in the locker room. She tries to look away, focuses on the hexagonal pink tiles, the swirls of hair that gather in the drain.

When she gets back to the apartment, Lou is lying on the floor beside the bathroom.

"Grandpa, what the fuck!"

"I'm okay," he says, and he winces, clenching his jaw.

"What happened?"

"I'm fine. I just slipped."

"I'm so, so sorry."

"I just need a little help getting up."

She grabs the walker from the living room and drags it down the long, carpeted hallway. She tries to lift Lou beneath his elbows but he moans at her touch.

"Fuck, fuck. Okay. We just need some help taking you to the hospital, okay? This'll be fine, I just don't know what I'm doing."

The EMTs are dressed in blue uniforms and look extremely capable. This is what they do every day, ten times a day. A ninety-three-year-old man falling is not scary to them, Alix thinks. They've probably seen people with knives wedged into their sternums, or brain matter spilling onto the sidewalk. This will be fine. Lou wails as they try to move him.

This is how it happens when people are old, she thinks. *The terminal event.* They take one step too quickly and break a bone and three days later they're delirious, being fed generic raspberry flavored Jell-O and whispering to their parents who died half a century ago. Her grandmother had been perfectly fine; she and Lou were on their way to pick up some books from the library on Seventy-first Avenue, when her grandmother lost her balance in the middle of the crosswalk. Less than a week later Alix sat beside her hospital bed and watched nurses swiftly change her diaper. Her grandmother's eyes were blank and her arms moved upward toward the ceiling. The gestures were slow and graceful, otherworldly.

A day later, Noah texts, *Yo, we on for tonight?*

"I can't stay long," she tells him when she gets to his house.

"That's cool. Wanna smoke a little?"

"Not really."

She holds Jamie's tote bag in her lap like a stuffed animal.

"You okay? You seem sort of tense."

"I'm fine."

"Uhh… you wanna watch something?"

"No, can we just have sex?"

"You betcha."

Outside, the sun is setting. The sky is a beautiful dreamy color—deep purples and blues, a spread of pink by the horizon. Water towers dot the buildings like their own little skyline. It's too tender a backdrop for this transaction.

"Can you turn off the lights?" Alix asks.

She's on top and moving vigorously to her own internal rhythm. She tries to stay focused but feels distracted by his presence—his hands gravitating toward her ass, his mouth against her breasts. It's like coming is a prize that she alone can win if she just concentrates.

"Stay still," she tells him. And she moves against him the way she would masturbate in college—mounting a pillow and muffling her moans into the crook of her elbow.

Just as she comes and an expanse of pleasure cracks open, she begins to weep.

Noah's voice is soft when he asks her what's wrong, if she's okay.

There's nothing to say, but she keeps crying, and what she feels is an emptying, a valve released. She's embarrassed but also indignant, fuck Jamie, she thinks, and fuck Noah too. Who is he to be the witness to her grief.

Lou isn't doing well. He says trolls are dancing on the ceiling of his room and he howls in pain when the nurses try to turn him. Alix's mother insists that he be transferred from the hospital on 66th Road to Cornell in Manhattan. Alix drives his car to the hospital today, just in case he's discharged. Never mind that yesterday, when she and her mother sat in the hospital cafeteria staring at unopened containers of yogurt, Nora said, unprompted: *Sweetie pie, he might not be coming home.*

There aren't any spots outside the hospital so Alix circles the block and makes a left on Second Avenue and then another on Sixty-eighth Street. There are so many fucking fire hydrants, even if an entire building of condos went up in flames there would not be a need for this many fire hydrants. She sees a man eating a perfectly frosted donut topped with coconut shavings and wants to slap it out of his hand.

On Seventy-third Street, which Alix has already driven down three times, there's finally a spot. She feels terrible for hating the donut man and she hopes there will never, ever be a fire. The space is tight but she can fit, it just might take a couple of tries. She's been emboldened by her grandfather's enthusiasm for her driving.

Alix backs up and cuts the wheel to the left. It's a bit too early, so she pulls out and does it again, this time over-correcting, waiting too long. She is maybe starting to hyperventilate. A man walks down the street and then stops beside her car, as if to watch her struggle. He's holding a green smoothie and absently scratching at a Band-Aid on his chin. The stream of cars has crossed the avenue and there's no one behind her; pulling out once again, she aligns herself with the car.

"Sweetheart," the guy says, "sweetheart, you're cutting the wheel too hard, ease up." She smiles at him, her heart beating rapidly.

"Please go fuck yourself," she says softly. She pulls out of the spot for the final time and makes a right onto Third Avenue, just as the light turns red.

Her phone buzzes in a cup holder which is still stained with her grandmother's coffee. Beside it is a pile of tissues and an opened packet of Dramamine, which Harriet needed whenever she was in the car, and which Alix can't bring herself to throw away. Now her head is aching and the red light seems impossibly long. She hopes her grandfather is asleep upstairs or foggy from the drip of morphine. Maybe Nora is sitting beside him, stroking his wrist absently as she reads the paper. Alix presses the heels of her hands into her eyes, hoping to relieve the pressure.

A few minutes later she does find a spot, but when she walks into the hospital lobby she isn't quite ready to be there. She sits on a bench and looks into her tote bag. A text from her mother: *ETA? Are you coming??*

Beside her on the tiled floor, two children play cards and shriek with delight as they race to slap a pile in the center. Their father is nearby on the phone and walking in slow, small circles. Alix walks through the atrium, pausing beside the muffins at the coffee cart; chocolate banana, cappuccino crunch, peach and walnut. She browses the gift shop and admires the fancy soaps, the stuffed penguins and bears, the lovely polished stones engraved with words like *PEACE* and *GRATITUDE*, *BREATHE* and CALM. She turns them over, one by one, so that only their smooth gray backs are visible.

WOMEN WHO RULE THE SCREEN

The woman sitting next to me on the train had pink hair and wore a bracelet made with small alphabet beads that spelled out *DEAD*DAD*CLUB*. She snored for most of the trip, but it was more meditative than disruptive. I was headed upstate to see my cousin Carly who'd had a baby a couple of months earlier. Her wife, Zoe, was a visiting professor at a liberal arts college along the Hudson, and they were there for the semester. I really wanted to meet the baby, but I also felt desperate to briefly sidestep the loneliness of my day-to-day life. I was no longer in a place where I could accurately say I was going through a breakup, and yet, I still *really* felt like I was going through a breakup.

Normally I loved taking the train; I didn't have to talk to anyone and nothing was expected of me, I could just read while being hurtled forward in relative silence. But I was hungover, and I winced when the sun shone, intermittently, through the dusty windows. The night before, I'd gone out for my friend Jackie's husband's birthday. Jackie's husband was kind of a tool but also really nice;

he was an I-banker, an expression I hadn't heard of prior to meeting him, but as Jackie liked to point out, he was also a budding philanthropist and mentored a boy whose mother was in prison.

We were at a bar in the West Village and I was waiting for my Negroni when an EDM cover of "Smells Like Teen Spirit" came on over the speakers. I bonded with the guy next to me who shook his head sadly and said something about Kurt Cobain rolling over in his grave. We went home together because all of my friends had gone home with their partners. He was a movie producer with thinning hair and a scar where there'd once been an eyebrow piercing. I remembered bits and pieces of the night; namely that he seemed like a real grown up because he had remote controlled window shades and a bar cart that held different kinds of whiskey. *Rich*, my friend Becky said. *You just mean he's rich.*

We made out on his leather couch and then he fingered me and I realized, with a flash of horror, that I'd forgotten to take out my *Ella*, the silicone cup that held my period blood.

"Dude, what is that?"

"Fuck, I'm sorry."

"Do you have a plastic pussy?"

"Something like that," I said and I hopped off the couch and adjusted my pants. I wasn't interested in explaining and then having him either a) smugly voice his support of my period and its related paraphernalia or b) express mild distaste for the situation and think of some reason to order me a car home. Recalling this on the train made me laugh out loud and I texted my group thread to share about my plastic pussy. Jackie responded immediately. *Omg. Guy's lucky it wasn't dentata down there.*

Carly and Zoe were almost a decade older—not my peers—and so their contentment was not something to disdain, it was aspirational. I'd seen Carly through her own mess of sorts: a stint of religious observance, and a period of disordered eating which may not have ever crossed over to an Eating Disorder proper, but still. And yet she'd arrived on the other side of forty with a graceful equilibrium. It was nice to be around.

I'd idolized Carly forever and at family functions I paid close attention to her ladybug studded earrings, a tortoiseshell hair clip, the Doc Martens she wore for years. She talked often of Ani DiFranco. Once I over-heard her say, *I'd rather date someone who cared about religion, any religion, even if it wasn't my own.* This struck me as wise and mature, and I was disappointed when I realized years later that I didn't actually agree with it.

I was still hungover and nursing a watery iced coffee when we pulled into the station. I tried to gather my belongings quietly so I wouldn't disturb my seatmate. My head throbbed as I bent to get my backpack from beneath the seat. Her eyes fluttered open and shut and she let out a soft belch.

Carly was waiting in the lot beside the station. Baby Louie, named after our Grandpa Lou, was in a car seat with a fist in his mouth. He had a huge, goofy grin on his face. Carly's breasts were enormous.

"You have a baby!" I cried.

"Sure do!" She was beaming, not harried with purple circles under her eyes like I'd expected. We hugged and she pulled back quickly.

It was late April and the first warm day in a while. I hadn't left the city in so long and I'd forgotten how clear and big the sky could be.

"I smell terrible," she said. "It's a thing, apparently. So

Louie can smell me. But it's still gross and I did shower yesterday, I promise." I squeezed her hand.

Carly and I had been at the supermarket when we learned over the radio that Eric Clapton's son had died. I was seven and I loved sucking on uncooked pasta straight from the box.

"Jesus fucking Christ," she'd said. It was the first time I'd heard her curse and I looked at her expectantly, waiting for her to apologize or blush, but she did neither. She'd grabbed two boxes of rigatoni and headed toward the register. People were murmuring on the check-out line. A woman held packages of frozen French fries and cried.

When we got back to my parents' apartment, a post-war high-rise near Lincoln Center, Carly had turned on the television and I'd poured a handful of pasta into my palm. Clapton's son was four-and-a-half and had fallen out the window of their fifty-third-floor apartment. We were on the tenth floor and our windows barely opened but I felt a flutter of panic and imagined myself tumbling out, soaring briefly before thudding onto the navy awning outside the lobby. Carly eyed me sucking on the pasta.

"You'll have to have some protein soon, okay? At least have a cheese stick or something?"

That particular weekend, Carly was babysitting because my parents were in Baltimore, moving my great uncle into an assisted living facility. He had Parkinson's and had lost most of his speech by that point. Sometimes he wrote me notes in big, loopy script. Whenever I saw him he'd take my hand and kiss it, his lips damp with drool. This was just a year before my parents split up, and I often think of it as the last intimate expression of their partnership.

That night, Carly's boyfriend Andy came over with Burger King: two Whoppers, a six-piece chicken tenders for me, and a large fries that we shared. We all agreed that the fries were inferior to McDonald's but ate them anyway. Andy wore baggy corduroy pants and a hoodie over his curly hair. We were listening to the classic rock station and Clapton's hits were on repeat: "Layla," "Bell Bottom Blues," some Cream songs.

"It's just so sad," Carly said again.

Andy was unmoved.

"I guess. That dude's super racist."

"I didn't know that."

"Well MTV probably didn't advertise it. He said some really awful shit a while back. Blamed it on being drunk, but you know that wasn't it."

"Okay, but it's still really sad."

"I suppose. But this is your problem, you really play into this idea of hero worship with celebrities. It replaces interpersonal relation with fixation on an illusion. And you don't actually think critically about why you're idolizing them."

"I don't *idolize* him," Carly said softly. A bouquet of plastic carnations collected dust on the dining room table and she brushed a finger along the petals.

"It's like the same way you romanticize 'Princess Di.' That she's so down to earth and empathetic and that the Royal Family's torching her—those're two sides of the same smug, entitled, neo-colonial coin."

Carly stood up and took a can of seltzer from the fridge. "Can we talk about this later?" she asked.

"Sure," Andy said. "So, Carly says your parents are in Baltimore this weekend?"

"Yup. My dad's from there," I told him.

"I was in Baltimore once when I was a kid," Andy said. "My parents took me to some indoor play space with friends of theirs and I pissed my pants in the ball pit."

I laughed and pieces of chewed up French fry came out of my mouth.

After dinner I sat on the sofa and braided and unbraided small sections of my hair, which was straight and brown but would become curly after puberty. My parents called to check in; my mom told me to brush my teeth before bed and reminded me to wash fruit before I ate it. I walked around the apartment with the cordless phone, surreptitiously looking at Carly and Andy. Things were tense but at one point I saw him put his hand in her back pocket.

On the last night Carly babysat, I was in my room when I heard her crying across the hall.

"Can you please stop?" she asked. "Why are you acting like this?"

I was going through a phase of reading young adult Holocaust fiction—stories about pre-adolescent girls forced from their homes, some to the Warsaw Ghetto and others into hiding.

"Seriously, I don't understand," I heard Carly say between sobs. "If you actually think that about me then you don't know me at all."

After she hung up, she came into my room and sat cross-legged on the carpet.

"He's allergic to me," she said, wiping her eyes with the back of her wrist. She began to cry again, her shoulders shaking uncontrollably. I felt ill-equipped to handle such emotion but moved that I was present for it. I held one of her hands and rubbed my thumb along her palm.

The phrase hung around idly in my thoughts for a long time. For a while I imagined that Andy broke into a rash when they touched, but as I got older it became obvious it was a metaphor, though I couldn't say for what.

Later that night, we got into my parents' king-sized bed and I braided Carly's hair while she read aloud from my favorite of the Holocaust books, about best friends in Denmark. One of the girls was Jewish and they pretended to be sisters in order to stay alive.

Carly and Zoe's house upstate was sweet and charming in a generic Airbnb and Pinterest sort of way—exposed shelving in the kitchen, lots of candles and mason jars, rugs with geometric prints. For dinner we got roasted chicken from the supermarket and Zoe sautéed spring beans and asparagus while Carly nursed Louie.

Louie snorted while he ate. Carly laughed and re-adjusted her nipple.

"You're a little piglet," she told him. She contorted her breast again, squeezed it at the base, and Louie latched like he was eating a hamburger.

"Let me pour you some wine," I said. I pulled out a bottle of rosé from my backpack, chosen from the $12-and-under table at the liquor store on Atlantic Ave. Zoe handed me a corkscrew.

"Can you please, please tell us something interesting?" she said. "We're painfully bored of talking and thinking about all this baby stuff. Sleep sacks and swaddles and nipple shields and a hundred different pumps."

"Literally just two pumps," Carly said. "But yeah, it's not particularly compelling. Please tell us things."

I poured us each a glass of wine. It was warm so I added a couple of ice cubes into the mason jars. I was so bored of myself I didn't know how to answer the question. All I thought about was the same stupid shit over and over again. My ex Jamie, other people I'd slept with or tried to sleep with or refused to sleep with. I thought of the time I went to see a therapist at student health my first year of college. I was unhappy and told her I wanted to transfer to Brown like everyone else I knew. She smiled smugly and said, "You know, you'll still be stuck with yourself wherever you are."

"I wish I had anything to share," I said now. "I did get a new job fairly recently, but Carly already knows." I told them about the historical society I was freelancing for, how I was working on an exhibit about tuberculosis in the late 19th century. The city had been ablaze with infection, spreading rapidly in part because of the architecture of the tenements. I'd been out of work for a while, and it felt good to be back, as if someone had taken out my batteries and flipped them around, like I used to do with the remote when I was a kid.

After dinner, I watched them give Louie a bath in a little turquoise tub. He squealed with delight each time they poured a cup of warm water over his belly or the top of his head. I made exaggerated faces at him and he smiled gleefully. I couldn't help but feel envious of him—how simple his needs were and that they were unequivocally met. Louie just wanted love reflected back at him, and he got it.

Carly and I sat on some wicker furniture on the screened-in porch while Zoe finished up the bedtime routine. I asked her how her brain felt. I told her I'd been expecting her to be anxious and overwhelmed but she seemed remarkably calm.

"Thanks," she said. "Yeah, I'm sure once I have to go back to work I'll have a meltdown, but I feel pretty even-keeled at the moment. Though I'm fucking exhausted all the time. It's like being on a red-eye from LA to New York, every single night."

Zoe came out holding a jar of weed in one hand and the baby monitor in another. Even though Carly wasn't smoking, she generously offered to roll us a joint.

"So, I hate to ask this question," Carly said, breaking the weed apart with her fingernails, "but are you dating? Still talking to Jamie? What's going on?"

I was both relieved and embarrassed that Carly had asked. Jamie and I hadn't spoken in many months. I blocked him on all social media but later I learned he was public on Venmo, and this was currently my only means of gathering information. Once he had given six dollars to someone named Jessica very early in the morning—a coffee cup emoji—clearly the result of a one-night stand. But more recently there were consistent payments between him and a woman named Lila: once the spaghetti emoji and then a taxi. It made me slightly queasy to see, but then I figured the relationship couldn't be *that* serious if they were still reimbursing each other for things.

"Nothing with Jamie in a while," I said. "I've been dating, I guess. Or like, seeing people here and there. I don't even really know how to talk about it. It all feels rather pathetic."

"You were together a long time! You can't expect to just shrug it all off quickly," she said.

I told them about some of the internet dates I'd gone on recently. Like the guy who was so nice but kept referring to Ray's Pizza on 4th Ave as a *pizzeria* and it drove me nuts. Another guy I was in bed with—extremely hot and scruffy in a '90s Ethan Hawke sort of way—who seemed promising until I discovered he had a Dave Matthews quote tattooed on his chest.

"Alix!" Carly exclaimed. "I had no idea you were such a judgmental little bitch."

"Have you met me?"

Zoe and I passed the joint back and forth. It was short and starting to get soggy.

"You know how periodically the Style section or *New York* mag will write an article about best friends raising a family together? 'Challenging the paradigm' or whatever? What if I just want that?" I said. "Why do I have to do all this stuff?"

"You don't have to," Carly said. "Come live with us."

The sun had been sinking slowly but suddenly the sky was dark, much darker than I was used to. Carly flicked on a porch light and Zoe played around with the baby monitor. The image was gray and pixelated and Louie was stirring. When he opened his eyes they lit up like a feral animal caught in the wild by a nature show.

"This is so random," I said. "But Carly, do you remember that weekend you stayed with me when my parents were in Baltimore with my dad's family?"

"Of course. And Eric Clapton's son died."

"Yes, exactly. And you and your boyfriend were fighting a lot. You were super upset, crying a ton and when I asked you what was wrong you said he was allergic to you."

"Huh." She slapped a mosquito that hovered above her thigh.

"Do you remember what that was about? For some reason it has lingered in my brain forever and I always wondered what it meant."

"No, I have no recollection of that at all. I don't even really remember him being around that weekend."

"Wow," I said. "That's wild. You were like, completely heartbroken."

That she could have been so devastated and no longer remember, this was not something I could understand. I wished so much that I was capable of forgetting, but it seemed my destiny to hold on to these sorts of things forever. Sometimes I wondered how my parents were able to rebuild after the divorce, how the undoing of our family wasn't the focal point of all our lives. For years they'd been regarding each other coolly, not openly hostile but cordial; there were periodic birthday or graduation dinners, and my father attended shiva after my grandfather died. He'd brought a platter of cookies and sat quietly in the living room of the Upper West Side apartment they'd once shared.

Intellectually, I understood my current despair probably had less to do with Jamie than it did my place in life, or rather the feeling of being behind, but it didn't *feel* that way. It felt shameful to be so consumed by a breakup and it didn't align with my understanding of myself: I'd gone to an all-women's college! My favorite category to watch on Netflix was *Women Who Rule the Screen*! I'd always prioritized my friends and family, was not one of those people who lost themselves in a relationship, who, as Carrie Bradshaw once said, had "committed the cardinal sin" of disappearing once partnered.

"Well, what's heartbreaking to me now," Carly said, "is that one day he'll just be that guy, the one you dated when Grandma died or the one who went to Thailand, whatever. You won't even remember! You don't believe me but it's true."

One by one, my friends had stopped shit-talking their partners. There was no longer talk of Jake's banana-shaped dick or of Anthony's boring finance job. The 11 a.m. texts on Sundays to meet up for bagels and a debrief of their evenings were replaced with *come hang out with us! Tim will make you brunch.* Allegiances were shifting. Even Becky, who historically would leave people's houses after fucking them and crawl into bed with me to watch Netflix, was often feeling *cozy at home* with her boyfriend. I felt desperate to be with Jamie, I did, but I still couldn't shake the idea that men were not my allies.

Zoe drummed her fingers absently against Carly's knee. My head suddenly felt heavy and my mouth was dry.

"I think I'm really high," I said and went inside.

Carly came in a few minutes later. She was wearing a nightgown and looked very Victorian. She handed me fresh pillowcases and a hand towel and we unfolded the couch together.

"I hope Louie doesn't wake you up," Carly said. "He stirs a lot and makes noises, but he's not upset so we try to ignore him. There are some earplugs in the bathroom if it gets bad."

"I'm not worried." I gave her a kiss and thanked her for taking care of me even though she had an actual baby to worry about.

I was used to hearing my neighbors walk from one room to another or the swell of an engine as a car raced south on Washington Avenue. The silence was unnerving and I was up for a long time. We'd left the bottle of rosé out on the table and eventually I finished what was left of it. Carly was right, Louie did babble a lot. He didn't seem upset, more like he was in conversation with himself. Both delighted and exhausted by his own sounds, a series of vowels strung together.

"Ah ooh," he said, like a little wolf pup. "Ah ooooh."

I recalled holding Louie earlier in the day, resting my chin on his small fuzzy head. The warm weight of him in my arms. I listened to the whir of the noise machine outside of the nursery and fell asleep.

Before I left, Carly packed me a peanut butter sandwich and a bag of baby carrots for the train. Louie was propped against a cushion and had two stuffed animals in his lap: a soft yellow duck and a blue whale with a sweet smile and a gleaming black button for an eye.

"Did you know," Carly asked, "that whales are the only mammals aside from humans that go through menopause?"

"I definitely did not know that."

"It's called the grandmother effect." She described the way that older maternal whales cared for their communities, how it had become so vital to their survival as a species, that it became part of the DNA. There was something solemn and beautiful about what she said, yet I felt desperate to get home, back to my life, even if it meant back to Becky and her dumb boyfriend, back to swiping and fucking guys with DMB tattoos, but before that, feeling the flicker of promise as I drank and flirted, conversed in a way that I knew was leading toward sex. I wanted to feel that moment just before it all shifted, when the night was still taut with possibility.

I gave Louie a kiss and told him he was a lucky boy.

ACKNOWLEDGMENTS

I am so grateful to Barbara Jones, whose keen editorial eye and encouragement have made this book the best version of itself.

Over the years many people have read and edited these stories. Thank you so much to Stephanie Clifford, Aja Gabel, Danielle Lazarin, Katie MacBride, Lee Pinkas, and Rebecca van Laer. I'm so grateful for the feedback from Rebecca Schiff and also from my mother, Marian Thurm. Thanks to George Axelrod for envisioning this book and its title many years ago.

Sam Axelrod has read these stories more than anyone ever should. Thank you, LYLAS.

I'm so grateful for the time I was able to spend at the Virginia Center for the Creative Arts and the Writing By Writers residencies.

To Christoph, Leza and Kaitlyn and everyone at CLASH, thank you for making this real.

Andrew, I'm so grateful you didn't end up in the pages of this book. I love you too.

ABOUT THE AUTHOR

Photo by Rose Lichter-Marck

Kate Axelrod's writing can be found in *Joyland, Narrative, Story* and various other publications. She studied Creative Writing at Oberlin College. She lives in Brooklyn with her husband and two children.

PREVIOUSLY PUBLISHED

Painkillers, *Barrelhouse,* February 2012

So Long, *New World Writing,* August 2015

I Did It, *Vol. 1 Brooklyn,* December 2015

My Father's Death Is a Law School Graduate, *Joyland,* July 2016

Comfort Pack, *7x7,* January 2017

A Third Party, *Cosmonauts Avenue,* May 2017

Both Joshes, *Vol. 1 Brooklyn,* December 2017

Their Exes' Exes, *Atticus Review,* January 2018 (Reprinted in *The Literary Review SHARE,* October 2020)

USB Port, *Hobart,* July 2018

At Full Capacity, *Joyland,* October 2018

Can You Please Tell Me What This Is Actually About, *Jellyfish Review,* November 2018

Making Things Up, *Narrative,* Spring 2021

Sex on Wednesdays, *Story,* Autumn 2021

ALSO BY CLASH BOOKS

EARTH ANGEL

Madeline Cash

SAD SEXY CATHOLIC

Lauren Milici

GIRL LIKE A BOMB

Autumn Christian

PROXIMITY

Sam Heaps

WITCH HUNT & BLACK CLOUD

Juliet Escoria

GENDER/FUCKING

Florence Ashley

GAG REFLEX

Elle Nash

I, CARAVAGGIO

Eugenio Volpe

AFTERWORD

Nina Schuyler

WE PUT THE LIT IN LITERARY

CLASHBOOKS.COM

FOLLOW US

FB

X

IG

@clashbooks

EMAIL

clashmediabooks@gmail.com

Printed in the USA
CPSIA information can be obtained
at www.ICGtesting.com
JSHW021427290424
62133JS00006B/224